Sex, Love, and Therapy

A Novel

David Rottman

Cover and book design: Maayan Laufer

Printed in the United States of America

ISBN-13 978-1-935184-04-1

Library of Congress Control Number:
2020930284

Published by:
Zahav Books Inc. Bronxville, New York

Contact: **info@zahavbooks.com**

Also by David Rottman

The Career As A Path To The Soul:
stories and thoughts about finding meaning
in work and life

For Hannah

"Do not awaken, nor stir up love, until its own time is due."
"I adjure you not to arouse love until its proper time."
"Swear to me you will not call up love before it is ready."
"That is, until it pleases."

--The Song of Songs, which is Solomon's 2:7, 3:5, 8:4

Chapter One

The Office of Dr. Yoav Zein. Psychotherapy.

Hours By Appointment.

Friday, October 29, 2010.

Considering that he was obsessed with his sex life, or rather the lack of one, it was remarkable that the episode that drove Jeff Smith into therapy involved his turning down an offer of sex from a woman he found deeply attractive.

On the day Jeff first came to my office, it was one of those lovely late October afternoons in New York when the sunlight is still warm, but there's a pleasant coolness underneath. My office is on the third floor of a Beaux-Arts building on Central Park West, overlooking the cross-town transverse and the park. Before my patients came that day, I opened the windows wide to enjoy the fresh air.

After he entered, Jeff looked around the office before sitting down. My patients and I sit facing each other on two white cotton sofas. There are framed photographs of Central Park on the walls, and a large teak cabinet with books and papers. Next to the patient's sofa, there is a box of tissues on a glass side table.

Jeff was quite tall, over six feet. He had sandy brown hair underneath a blue baseball cap with no logo. As he sat down, he tossed a red and black hunter jacket on the sofa and asked, "What do we do here?"

"We can talk about whatever's on your mind," I said.

"I'm messed up," he said. "That must be a good enough reason for doing this."

In that first session, I learned that Jeff worked as a circulation editor for an online newsmagazine, a job he had fallen into without much planning. The pay was good, he said, and the work was easy enough, but he had no idea if he would stay in the job or where it might lead him.

"I don't like to think about the future," he said.

"How come?"

"It might not be what I want it to be."

Jeff said he rented a studio apartment on the West Side near Columbia on a month-to-month basis, although the landlord had offered a one-year lease. He grimaced when he said the apartment smelled vaguely of mold, and the gas jets were old and leaked a bit. He told me all this quickly, then scratched the stubble on his cheeks, paused, and said, "Look, maybe it would be a good idea to talk about my job and the future later on, but I really want to talk about something else."

The something else was his account of what happened in August on the annual fishing and camping trip he took with four of his college friends, and their wives and girlfriends, on the Madison River in Montana.

On the first day of the trip, Jeff and his best friend Mike Comorks had a moment alone without the others, wading and casting their flies sidearm into the quiet but quickly flowing West Fork of the river. Then Mike started talking and said his marriage to his wife, Noel, was falling apart at the seams. "All we do is fight all day long," Mike said. He turned to Jeff with a steely look in his eyes. "I hope you know what a bitch she is." As Mike spoke, Jeff looked away and felt something snap inside him. Noel seemed like the ideal woman to him, and he was stunned by the fact that anyone, and especially Mike, could be so coldly critical. From that moment on, Jeff avoided Mike in the camp, making sure that he and Mike were never alone again. He found he couldn't look directly at Noel either.

On the last night of the trip, Mike produced four bottles of different brands of tequila at dinner. After eating, everyone got "ripped" as they sat close to each other around a large stone fire ring until late, tasting the liquors, laughing and shouting into the crisp night air. Jeff didn't have a current girlfriend, and after the others went to bed, he sat around the embers of the campfire in the dark, roasting the last marshmallows by himself. He was highly aware of what was going on in the other tents spread out under the vast Montana sky. For the first few nights, he was irritable about being alone, but during the days his mood lifted and, out on the water, he was exuberant about the marvelous sparkle of the river.

Early the next morning, the others got in their canoes and went far down river to try a last fishing spot. Jeff declined the offer to join them. He'd finished several half-full bottles by himself the night before and was feeling tired and "wasted."

After the others were gone, he dismantled his tent but crawled back into his sleeping bag. Lying on his back, surrounded by thin, narrow-crowned lodgepole pines, he chewed on the stem of a pink long-leafed phlox while dragonflies buzzed around his head. Staring into the cloudless blue sky, he forced himself to think about what could be waiting for him back home. Thoughts about the future tended to buzz around like the insects.

Jeff was startled by a rustling behind him, and he realized someone was there. He turned his head sharply and saw the face of Noel as her wet hair brushed his face. She slid into the sleeping bag and he felt with a jolt that she was naked. She was giggling as she pressed herself against him. Her skin was cool as she had just come out of the river.

He sat up. "What're you doing?" he asked.

"I told the others I'd catch up with them. You looked like you needed me."

"What do you mean?" Jeff was intensely aroused.

Noel smiled as she put her arms around Jeff and tried to pull him on top of her.

"No," Jeff said and pushed her arms away. Shaking his head, he said, "Noel, not like this."

Noel unzipped the top of the sleeping bag and showed herself to him. "Honey," she said, "I want you." Her wet hair was draped over her shoulders and the skin on her body was tight with small bumps from shivering.

"Oh God, you are so…" He was breathing hard and his voice was shaky. "Not like this. No. Jesus." He looked away.

"I thought you wanted me." Noel's voice was full of disappointment.

"I do. There's nothing I want more. But not like this, Noel. Not with you and Mike needing to work things out."

"You don't have to stop because of Mike. He and I are through." She was beginning to cry. "I know about his screwing around. I thought if I ignored it, he would get over it. Now we both know the marriage was a mistake from the beginning." Noel looked at Jeff and said, "You have so much more to offer than he does." She reached for him again.

Jeff jumped up out of the sleeping bag. "No," he said, more loudly. "Noel, no." He was almost shouting. "We can't. No." He turned his back to her, opened his kit bag, found a towel, turned back to her, and threw her the towel. "Go get dressed," he said. As he walked away, he said, "I'm making breakfast."

Twenty minutes later he and Noel were eating eggs and the last of the stale bacon and talking awkwardly about the trip. When the others arrived at lunch, there were a few jokes about the stragglers being alone in camp, but the incident passed with no more being mentioned.

After the trip was over, Mike was away for several weeks. Then late one night Jeff received a phone call from Mike, who had been drinking. Mike was calling with the news that he and Noel had agreed on a divorce and were already living apart. Mike rambled on about how much he hated Noel. "I only married her because you liked her," Mike said bitterly.

Jeff was shocked. "Me? Are you crazy? You chased after her like she was the last woman in the world."

"Why the hell do you think I did it, asshole? Because you thought she was so hot."

Jeff's shock was complete. He had no idea that he had played such a role in Mike's pursuit of Noel. "You can have her now, buddy boy," Mike said as he was about to hang up. "But you'd better get your shots first."

With that, Jeff abruptly stopped recounting what happened on the trip, took off his baseball cap, ran his hands through his hair, and looked at me with a puzzled expression. "It's all so strange. I've been replaying everything that happened in college, over and over again, to check if I missed something."

"And what have you come up with?" I asked.

"It seems like everything that had happened back then wasn't what I thought it was. Mike was my best friend. We were really close. The first year in college, we did each other's class assignments. We ate most of our meals together. He even used to wear my high top sneakers. Now we don't talk to each other. How could something like that happen?" He looked down and added more quietly, "I guess I could've seen it coming. Maybe I didn't want to."

Jeff said the strain in their friendship began in recent years with Mike's frequent tales of his "sex adventures." After Mike's marriage to Noel, the endless stories of his extramarital escapades made Jeff uneasy. Mike took long and sometimes unnecessary trips supervising his sales team for a computer parts company. He frequently told Jeff in detail how he "fooled around" with the available women he was always able to find at airport bars and in hotels.

The knowledge of Mike's infidelities made Jeff extremely uncomfortable. "It got to be where sometimes I made excuses not to be around the two of them," he said. Noel seemed oblivious, but Jeff did notice over time that her drinking had increased. She was drinking on a par with Mike, who was buying a bottle of Scotch almost every day to go along with many beers. As Mike's lurid stories became more graphic and his sex episodes grew more frequent, Jeff wondered if he should tell Noel about her husband's philandering.

"I asked myself, why did he always have to tell me all this stuff with women? Did he want me to be the one to tell Noel? I don't know. Anyway, he never said to tell her, and she never asked about it." In the end, Jeff said, he placed loyalty to his friend as a first consideration and kept quiet. "So you're probably wondering why I didn't do it with Noel, right?"

"So why didn't you?"

"I wish I knew. She's a big part of the reason I came here."

"What do you mean?"

"I thought she was what I wanted. I've been hot for her for years." Jeff said he was the first to have met Noel when they were in college at Columbia. She sat next to him in Applied Macroeconomics, and he found he couldn't concentrate on the lectures. He used to make his way early to class, eager to get a glimpse of her. She'd stroll slowly down the Van Am quad at the university. She knew she was being watched and she liked it. Telling Mike about her, Jeff described her as his idea of what an attractive woman should look like. "Everyone says she's got a great figure, but that's not what always got to me. It's her blue-green eyes. They're very intense. When she looks at you, all you can see is how big her eyes are. That turned me on."

Jeff said his preoccupation with Noel kept up after the years in college. Even after she was married, he often paid her compliments ("whoa, who is looking good today!"). There was an on-going joke among the group that Jeff was smitten with her and that was why he hadn't married yet. Jeff blushed at the jokes, but Noel only smiled, and he was pleased by the fact that she didn't reject their implications.

"Mike never seemed to mind," Jeff said, "he wouldn't say anything, he'd just roll his eyes. I guess I thought things with all of us would just go on the same way forever. I never imagined things could crack wide open."

Finishing his account of what happened after the trip, he said, "About a month later I did get one last phone call from Mike in the middle of the night. He was roaring drunk and wanted to introduce me to a woman he'd picked up at the bar where we were regulars. This time he was fooling around with someone in our own neighborhood. I had this awful sick feeling about it. He said, 'C'mon over, there's a party girl here for both of us.' I yelled at him to sober up and go home. The next day I got a call from Noel. She said Mike left early that morning for another business trip and she was all alone. She wanted to know if I would like to come over for a drink after work? She needed to see me. I said no because I had to work late. I didn't feel good about either one of those calls."

Shaking his head back and forth, he said, "Mike seems like a totally different person to me now. I'm not sure I even like him anymore. What's there to like about a guy who calls you at three in the morning when he's drunk and curses you out for his own decision to marry his wife? What can you say to such a person?" Shaking his head, he said, "Mike was like a member of my family, he was such a part of my life, but I think now my friendship with him is over. It's crazy how nothing's what it seemed. It's just unreal."

"This is difficult to take in."

"It is. And the weirdest thing is I can't bring myself to call Noel, not even to send my regrets about the break-up. Before the trip, I was a slave to how much I thought I wanted her."

"But not now?"

"Sometimes I don't think I'm normal. I spent all those years daydreaming about getting my hands on her. Now she's free, and I don't want to be involved with her at all." He was shaking his head again. "That's today, anyway. On other days I waver."

As our first session drew to a close, Jeff seemed to realize he had talked almost uninterruptedly for nearly an hour. He stopped abruptly and asked, "What do you think about all this?"

"I think you can get something very valuable from these events."

"You do?"

"Yes, I think the important events of our lives can reflect things back to us. Things we need to know about ourselves."

"Like what?"

"You had a desire for someone you didn't love."

"Wow. I guess I did say that, didn't I?" For just a moment, Jeff seemed fully present, fully engaged in the moment between us. He asked, "Where does something like that come from?"

"That's something we can talk about here."

"You're right. I guess that is something to talk about. I don't have any idea what it's like to desire someone you love." Then as we both stood and he put on his red and black jacket, the present moment slipped away and he was back in the past. As we walked to the door, he said, "The only thing I know now is I must've been crazy for stopping it. All this time I was on fire for her. And then there she was in my sleeping bag, all wet and slick, reaching for me. God, she looked so fantastic. And I have to go and say no. I'll probably regret it the rest of my life."

Chapter Two
The Office of Dr. Grace Brennan. Psychotherapy.
Hours By Appointment.

Friday, October 29, 2010.

As a woman doing therapy, I was often asked by friends and
relatives and even by male colleagues, isn't there a difference in
therapeutic approach between a man and a woman? As a woman,
wasn't I more likely than a man to be moved by the patient's pain?
Wouldn't I be more gentle? Those seemed like innocent questions, but
then they were always followed by a zinger. As a woman, did I think I
would be as capable of helping with problems of a more serious
nature? I couldn't help noticing that my male colleagues were never
asked such questions. But nevertheless, I always gave my best
answer. Would I offer more comfort than a man? Not necessarily, I
often replied. As much as I might want to help, I knew not to spare
the pain that was necessary to reach a goal.

In that regard, I often think of Michelle M., as she called herself. It
wasn't a good prognosis that Michelle was quite late for our first
session. She sat down on the sofa, crossed her legs, and glared at me.

She was an attractive looking young woman, soon to be thirty years old, but she appeared younger than her actual age. She was wearing a low-cut grey chiffon crisscross blouse and an above the knee black double slit skirt.

I waited as she crossed her legs back again. A few minutes passed. Silence.

Then Michelle's face began to quiver. The tough pose she put on vanished. Instead, there was the face of a confused and very uncertain young woman.

"I don't know where to begin," she said.

I waited again.

At last, Michelle sighed. "I'm bored."

"Tell me more about that," I said.

In that first session, Michelle talked about the circumstances of her life, her boyfriend, and her large family. Michelle was from the privileged class. She seemed to have every advantage that anyone could ask for: she was intelligent, pretty, and came from a wealthy and politically prominent family. She had friends from many walks of life. However, two things didn't seem to work out well in her life: men and her career.

As she talked, she got up from the sofa and walked around my office. I put a lot of myself into that office. Twenty years before, I'd been lucky to buy my share of a three-office suite, just off of Lexington Avenue on the East Side. I'd furnished the office with chenille curtains, a long velour slate-gray sofa, and two silver-gray loveseats from a Venetian designer. They almost matched Michelle's blouse. On either side of the sofa, there were contemporary aqua lamps and floating bookcases. Whatever my patients might feel in such a feminine environment, I was the one who spent my days there, and I wanted to be comfortable.

Some patients never left their seat, but Michelle walked over to a long walnut table where I put many things I collected over my travels, painted jewelry boxes from Ecuador, ceremonial masks from West Africa, glass paperweights from the Southwest. She picked up a small translucent hand-blown pumpkin and turned it over in her hands.

"Do you like your work?" she asked.

"I do. And do you?"

"No, I hate it. I'm a temp. I want to do something else."

"What kind of work you want to do?"

"I want to be an actress."

"Have you studied?"

"Yes, I went to acting school for two years, and I've got a private drama coach. But I don't want to be just any kind of actress."

"What do you mean?"

"I want to be an improvisational actress in the avant-garde theater."

"That's very specific. How did that develop?"

"So you're skeptical?"

"I am?"

"You're just like all the rest, you mock people. My mother mocks me. My boyfriend mocks me too."

I noted the bait and ignored it for later.

"He mocks you?"

"Yeah, he says like 'What? Making a living as a regular actress isn't hard enough already?'"

"Are you making a living from your temp work?"

"That's a laugh."

"So how do you get by?"

"I get the interest from a trust fund my grandmother left me."

Michelle sat down as she told me the Machmad family was wealthy, but the money from the trust fund was all she got from them. There was just enough money to cover the rent on her small apartment, just a few blocks away on the East Side. She sighed as she said, "There's a bit left over for clothes, a little passion of mine. And for my acting coach. He's supposed to help me with my auditions."

"Oh, you go on auditions?"

"A few." She sighed. "Not many lately."

"How come?"

"I'm not what they're looking for, at least that's what I'm told."

"That sounds difficult."

"Uh, yeah, what do you think?"

Again, I noted the bait. "So what else do you do?" I asked.

"Like I said, I'm a temp. A receptionist. I don't type."

We talked about temping, how the change in the work atmosphere every few weeks or months was a relief from the boredom of doing phone work. Unlike some other temps, Michelle had never been offered a permanent job from any of her assignments.

"How come?" I asked.

"The temp agency says I have 'indifferent work habits.' Sometimes, I'm short with customers on the phone. Sometimes I don't pick up the phone when it rings."

"Oh, why is that?"

"I don't know…something just comes over me. It just seems easier to put up with the ringing than listen to another voice in my ear."

"Is there any other reason you haven't gotten a permanent job?"

"I was told I'm a distraction to the other workers. You know, the guys."

"What guys?"

"The guys who keep bothering me. They're always hanging around, chatting me up at my desk."

 "Do you have trouble putting them off?"

"No way."

Michelle said one such "suitor" took too many liberties recently. He was a young man who already had an impressive executive title. When he made a few flirtatious remarks that were a bit smutty, she thought he crossed the line. In the presence of many others, she told him, "Get lost, mister big shot." She laughed as she recalled this episode. She had a brittle laugh that came from the top of her throat, and when she was particularly amused, she would "hoot," as she put it.

"Enough about work," she said. "Can I talk about men?"

"We can talk about whatever is on your mind."

"I'm going out with a guy who's an impresario. He's a nightlife kind of a guy. My sisters call him a hustler. They think I only date hustlers. He's actually not like that, he's much more of a businessman than you'd think. He goes on and on about money. I hate listening to him." She looked down at her outfit and added, "I don't look like this when I go out."

"Oh, what do you look like?"

"I've got the shortest leather mini-skirt you've ever seen." Michelle stood up to show with her hands how far up the mini-skirt went. She said her boyfriend bought her fishnet stockings and the mini-skirt and a black and red leather bustier to wear to the nightclub where he produced acts. But then she complained, "once we get there, he's always working so I have to spend my time at the bar. It's so boring."

She looked at me with what I would come to know as her "drop dead" look. "You probably think I drink. Well, I don't. I'm a health nut. It's just Perrier for me."

I wondered at that moment if Michelle already saw me as an unsympathetic Mom, and I made a mental note not to let that possibility derail the therapy.

"So your boyfriend is boring, and work is boring?"

"You got it. Sometimes it gets so bad I have blasts at work."

"What are those?"

"I suppose you'd call them tantrums."

"Tantrums?"

"I just feel so smothered. Like today. It's unbearable."

"What happened today?"

"Nothing special, same as what happened yesterday and the day before."

Michelle said that when work got particularly tedious, when the feeling of being stifled and smothered became simply intolerable, she would bang the telephone down on the reception desk and say, "I'm bored, Bored, BORED." This was followed by "I'm bored Out-Of-My-MIND." The tantrums were worst in the midweek when she didn't have a date to look forward to in the evening. Then she would rant and rave, "I hate my job, I hate my life, I can't stand it anymore. I'm bored out of my everlovin' skull."

"Are people surprised when you do that?"

"Nah, they usually just keep away."

"Does anyone offer any sympathy?"

"I don't like sympathy."

"I see. Do these blasts help?"

"No, not really."

Michelle shifted about on the sofa, as if searching for a comfortable perch, then gave up on the effort and screwed up her face. "This isn't going to work, is it?"

"Why do you say that?" I asked.

"Because you just sit there and don't say anything. I can't stand that. You're just like all the rest, you get your jollies from listening to problems all day long and then you get a fat check."

"Michelle, I don't listen to problems. I listen to people."

She looked at me for a moment, then threw back her head, spread her legs out sideways and hooted.

I leaned toward her. "Michelle, you must listen carefully to what I'm about to say. My view is that the way forward for you is going to require some very serious work, some very difficult work. It will require both our best efforts. I will do everything I can on my side. But you will also have to pull your share of the weight at all times. Only you can decide if you are willing and able to undertake something as challenging and difficult as this enterprise. I want you to give some thought to what I've said before you decide whether to continue working."

Michelle glared at me. It was the end of the session, and she left without saying goodbye. Still, she did call for an appointment for the next week. But when she returned, late again, she immediately started to berate me.

"I'm furious at you," she said. "You scared the hell out of me last week. I was a wreck when I left here. You ought to have the decency to recognize that people are in a vulnerable position when they come to see you."

"What are you vulnerable about?"

"I'm vulnerable...I'm vulnerable..." Michelle was spluttering. "I'm vulnerable..."

I waited.

"To you if you tell me I'm fucked up."

"That's the difficult task I talked about last week," I said. "You will have to submit yourself to this process, to the work, and to me and my role in it. That will include feeling very vulnerable at times."

After a period of silence, tears rolled out of Michelle's eyes while she looked straight ahead. "Are you sure you're not crazy like all the rest?"

There was a long moment when we just looked at each other.

"I'm not sure I know what you're talking about at all but I want to try it," she said at last. "What am I supposed to do?" she asked.

I told her of the procedures for the sessions, including the fact that she would be charged for the sessions whether she came or not. Pulling her weight would also include showing up on time.

She asked, "What do you want me to talk about today?"

"What do you feel like talking about?"

"I feel like complaining."

"What about?"

"How bored I am."

"It's very painful, isn't it?"

Michelle looked down and wept.

After five minutes, a very long time to cry, she looked up and said,

"I'm sorry to take up your time like this."

"This is your time, Michelle."

"But you won't want me to come back if I keep crying."

I was silent.

"Maybe you want to know why I'm crying?"

Once again, I was silent.

As if to reassure herself, she asked, "Are you sure you're not like all the rest?"

"Michelle, you've said that more than once. What's this about 'all the rest'?"

It seemed that Michelle had two previous episodes in therapy, both arranged by her father. Both were male psychiatrists who prescribed the use of mood-altering drugs. Michelle refused and spent the time in protracted arguments with her psychiatrists.

"They always have to win," she said. "They're always right."

"It's too bad they weren't," I said.

"I wanted them to know better than I did."

Michelle said she felt "reduced to nothing" by the way the psychiatrists had "misused their authority" in the arguments that had taken place. She was quite honest in saying she was afraid that was about to happen again. And she was disturbed and frightened by the way one of the psychiatrists had abandoned his professionalism and responded to her seductively.

"Maybe it's good that you're a woman therapist," she said.

"I'm very sorry you went through that," I said.

"Wait a minute, you are?"

"I really am."

"You don't want to argue with me about it?"

"No, not at all."

"Huh. You're the only one who doesn't want to argue with me."
She added, "I come from the house of arguments."

Michelle went on to tell me about her childhood home, a place
where her mother and father were united with a compelling message
to her: don't be like everyone else in the family, don't shout and don't
argue. "Daddy," as she called him, was a "massively handsome man."
He was one of the most notable corporate heads in the country. The
business press described his tenure in charge of a media conglomerate
as one that had led to "unparalleled growth through acquisitions and
diversifications."

"Mother" was a society hostess who "policed" her three daughters,
especially Michelle who was the youngest. Mother was the
"choreographer" of Daddy's career. She made the moves behind the
scenes that led later to his political career. In the same article in the
business press about her father, her mother was described as a woman
whose upswept hairdo looked like she "wore a permanent tiara."

To her parents, Michelle said, the children were a little needed part
of the background choreography. "You're the youngest. Be the darling
and be obedient," her father often told her, "not like your sisters." Her
mother often said, "If you don't dress up, you won't look good
alongside your sisters." And even more often, her mother said,
"Michelle, you know how I love it when you look nice."

"As far as my parents are concerned, I'm a possession," Michelle
said, "like their houses and their cars. Like my mother's jewels." She
rolled back her head and hooted. "Only I don't need dusting."

"How do you deal with that?" I asked.

"I don't," she said.

"What do you mean?"

"They say I'm the only one who doesn't like to fight in the open, but I still get my message across."

"What message?"

"They say I don't deserve any credit for not shouting or arguing because I do everything I'm asked with a bad attitude. I call myself Michelle M., they call me Michelle R. They do it even in front of other people."

"Why do they do that?"

"It's a dig. The R is for resentment."

Michelle said her two older sisters were always shouting, so much so that the house was often in an uproar. They had rebelled with drinking and drugs, car crashes and shoplifting arrests, and fierce arguments that went all over the house and even outside. Unlike those two, Michelle craved peace and often hid in her room. She cooperated with what her parents wanted, but with resentment that was unmistakable. Her mother often frowned at Michelle's choice of clothes and friends, and her sisters often frowned at her desire to avoid open conflict with her parents.

"The only one on my side was Mimi."

"Mimi?"

"She was my dog."

Mimi was Michelle's elegant black flat-coated retriever. Michelle said that Mimi, like many in her breed, never grew up and kept her puppy-like temperament even when full grown. They took long walks together through the woods on the estate of her family's home in "horse country" in New Jersey's Somerset County. Michelle's bond with Mimi carried her through some of the unhappy years of her childhood.

"Mimi was supposed to be the family dog, but really she was my dog. I made her mine."

"How did you do that?"

"We got her when I was eight. When she was about a year old, we were all in back of the house, playing fetch with her with a big stick. The stick went into the brambles and she went after it. She started howling. The most God-awful sound. She had a big thorn stuck right in her paw. She wouldn't let us get near her. Even Daddy didn't know what to do. They were all just watching and she was terrified. I couldn't stand it. So I just ran and put my hand over her muzzle and laid her on my lap and stroked her head. I was crying my eyes out and then I just pulled out the thorn, very slowly. And you know what happened then?"

"She became your dog?"

"No, that was later. She bit me. Hard. I had to have stitches. That was a big shock, but I learned something from it."

"What did you learn?"

"That I loved her even if she bit me. That's when she became mine."

We sat in silence for a very long time.

The raw impact of what she said hovered in the air. In the space between us now was pain and courage, acquiescence and defiance, all mixed together. I felt as though the journey of her life had arrived in the room, full of weight and consequence. We had reached the end of the session. In the strongest way, I felt called upon to respond to her, for the possibility that healing could make its first appearance.

"So you can love," I said.

Michelle's eyes widened and she looked at me as if seeing me for the first time. As we walked to the door, she said, "You know that about me?"

Chapter Three—Jeff

The Office of Dr. Yoav Zein.

Hours By Appointment.

Friday, November 19, 2010.

As the weather grew colder during the first weeks of November, I continued seeing Jeff, but nothing seemed to be helpful at this point. He began most of his sessions by holding his sides and saying, "I feel so messed up." Over and again he revisited the sleeping bag episode and the vision of Noel that haunted him. The loss of his friendship with Mike and the shattering of his daydreams about Noel had "turned his world upside down."

"Despite everything, I still want to touch her," he said, as much to himself as to me. "It's the worst when I try to sleep. I turn out the lights, climb in bed, close my eyes, and there she is, naked. She shows herself to me and she says, 'I want you.' It's like a goddam broken record. And I can't stop wondering what it would feel like to do it with her." He stared at his open hands and hardly seemed present in my office.

There is a prerogative for a therapist to change the direction of the conversation to help the progress of the work, but of course it's one that must be used with care. With Jeff, these moments came frequently at the beginning.

"What's going on in your life now?" I asked. "Do you have plans for Thanksgiving?"

"I'll spend it alone. I don't want to see my family or my friends and I sure don't feel like there's much to be thankful for." Jeff put his hands to his sides. He looked directly at me. "I should probably tell you something. This thing with Noel is just one more frustration. It's not that new."

"What does that mean?"

"With sex, it always seems to amount to the same thing."

"The same thing?"

"There was this girl named Ellen when I was in high school. She was like a ripe peach in all the right places. It was late on a Saturday night and we were down in my basement on the old couch and my parents were upstairs. I was unhooking her bra and about to get to the holy of holies when my mother came halfway down the stairs. She said, 'Jeff, it's getting late. It's time to take Ellen home.' So Ellen scrambled into her blouse and we went upstairs and said goodnight to my parents and I drove her home. Then she moved away and I never saw her again. Frustration."

"You said it always seemed to amount to the same thing?"

"I never seem to get where I want to go, it's always been like that in life. Something steps in and stops me."

"Something steps in?"

"It's like a higher power."

"So you know what it's like to meet a higher power?"

"I suppose."

"But that isn't helpful?"

"No, not at all. I know you're supposed to welcome obstacles, they're there for you to get stronger. I've thought a lot about that. Maybe it's true for other people, but I don't relate to that. I mean, I don't think I ever got anything from struggling. Like with Noel, there wasn't anything positive that came out of it. There never is."

"That's been your experience."

"Yeah, with me, it's just one frustration after another. Sometimes I think sex was put on earth just to torture me. It was like that with Ellen and everyone else." Jeff took off his baseball cap and twisted it as he spoke. "Ok, so maybe it wasn't the right time and the right place with Ellen, but then there was this girl Margery. I was still in high school and her parents were away for the weekend. She called me over and we were kissing on the floor and she put my hand down her pants. Then she moved my hand and said 'there, do it there' and I did it there and she started moaning. Then I took her hand to put it down my pants and she sat up like a shot and said 'I don't do that.' Then she wanted me to do it to her again. It's like I'm always getting a message, only it's not a message I like getting."

"What do you think the message is?"

"You know I thought about it a lot. I mean, a real lot. I was thinking about it just before Noel jumped into my sleeping bag. The message is about everything in my life, not just about sex. It's about not getting what I want. Something always seems to trip me up. Maybe that's the real reason why I came to see you."

"What do you think trips you up?"

"Who knows? Maybe I'm afraid to find out." Jeff was silent for a long moment. "Anyway, with Noel, I have to admit it wasn't Mike that stopped me. He probably would've been thankful if I'd gone ahead and done it with her. I think he would've been relieved."

"So it wasn't for his sake that you stopped," I said.

"No, I guess not."

"Then why did you?"

"I'm not sure. I guess I've got outdated notions of chivalry."

"What makes them outdated?"

"Well, everybody else thinks I'm off the wall for not having done it with her. Even some of my women friends think I was nuts. They're actually mad at me."

"You're wondering if their attitude is the right one for you?"

"I suppose I am, but how can I know? Maybe it is, maybe it isn't." He looked pained. "What makes anything right?" Jeff looked down.

"Let's go back for a minute. What's your definition of `chivalry'?" I asked.

"You know. Chivalry." He shrugged.

"What does it mean to you?"

"I guess in this case it means only doing it when it's right."

"Yes. And why?"

"So I can feel proud of myself, I guess." There was a change in Jeff's voice. "Pride, pride, pride," he said.

"Pride? Is that an issue for you?"

"It's an issue in my whole family."

"What do you mean?"

"It was my Dad's thing. He was all about pride."

Jeff went on to explain that his father was the strong, silent type.

Jeff went to his office in a suit and sometimes even wore a tie, while his father had always worn auto mechanics overalls to work. His father's repair shop did well because he was a man of unquestioned integrity. Customers stayed with him for decades. He was stern and gruff but "honest as the day is long." While Jeff was growing up, his father's advice was rare and as brief as it was simple. "Always do your best. Let your work speak for itself." Jeff seldom discussed much with his father; their conversation was limited to the outdoors and to sports.

"My Mom said Dad was a man who lived by a code."

"What was that?"

"Keep your mouth shut, suck it up, deal with it, and don't make a fuss. Don't ask for help. You don't need anybody to tell you if you've done your best, you know yourself. Don't let anyone know your private business. Stuff like that. He was better at it than anybody I've ever met. The truth is, I've always felt like less of a man because I couldn't just suck it up the way he did. But then I suppose that's what did him in at the end."

"At the end?"

"He died of a perforated ulcer in my first year of college. I found out they saw him doubled over in the morning at the repair shop, but he wouldn't let them drive him to the emergency room. At lunch he got into his own car by himself and headed up to the hospital. He pulled off to the side of the road a few blocks before he got there. That was where they found him when he didn't come home at night. Slumped over the wheel."

Jeff stared at the floor in silence. I waited for him to resume speaking. After a few minutes, he looked up, blinked a few times, and said, "The thing about Dad was, he wasn't anybody ever but himself. Nobody ever saw him act differently than he was." He added, "Nobody ever saw him have doubts...like me."

"So you think less of yourself because of your doubts?"

"I do. I'm not as tough as my Dad was."

"Maybe you and your father had different ways of dealing with doubts."

"I always felt like his way was better."

"You don't think he had doubts?"

"Maybe. But if he did, nobody ever knew about them." Jeff was thinking hard again. "You know, now that we're talking about this, I can see that he couldn't picture himself trusting the people in the emergency room. It really did kill him." After he weighed what he had just said, he added, "He didn't want to have to put himself in other people's hands."

"That was part of his code?"

"No doubt." Jeff blew out a breath of air. "Hah, there's that word again. Doubt."

It was the end of the session and there were many things left sore and open. In the following session Jeff entered quickly, tossed off his hunter coat, slipped off a grey sweater, sat, and continued where we left off as if no time had passed between sessions.

"I've been thinking a lot about what it meant to me to have a father who never showed he had any doubts."

"And?"

"It kind of left me on my own."

I nodded.

"I guess I've got to make my own code. Like when we talked about chivalry?"

"Can you say more?"

"I was thinking, maybe it's my own code that makes me do things like toss a naked woman out of my sleeping bag."

I waited for him to continue.

"The thing is, the code never gives me a break. It's always testing me."

"It's testing you?"

"It's like the code is always throwing obstacles in my way, like it wants to see if I can raise the bar. I'm always fighting it."

"You're having a battle with your code?"

"Right. I think that's why I couldn't go along with my friends who think I should've had sex with Noel. They don't see there's something going on in me about needing to raise the bar. Maybe I was just trying to get to my own code, like my father did. I mean there must have been a reason I passed on something that hot." He looked again at his hands. "So what is that bar? The one I started to raise when I didn't do it with Noel."

"Do you have an idea?"

"No. Do you?"

"It sounds like the bar is your concept, and your practice, of what it means to be a man, on your own terms."

"What does that mean?"

"With Noel you were saying to yourself, in effect, that there are some things you wouldn't do."

"The circumstances weren't right."

"Yes. You have some criteria that weren't being met."

"I guess I'm not like Mike. There are some things I won't do." Jeff was smiling. "Some things I just don't do." After a pause, he asked, "Why is it so damned important to have a code?"

"Well, I don't think it's just because your father had one."

"What do you mean?"

"It's more primal than that. The thing about human beings is, we don't have instincts that automatically tell us how to behave. We need other things, like your code, to govern our behavior. We have to know that about ourselves."

"Know what?"

"That we don't have to obey our impulses."

"I don't get it."

"You majored in biology, right?"

"Yes."

"You know how biologists define an instinct?"

"It's a pattern of behavior that isn't learned. It's innate."

"That's right. So we don't have an instinct that tells us exactly how to live, how to be a man. We have to learn a lot of it."

"Even with sex?"

"Especially with sex."

"But my Dad always seemed to know his code. It didn't seem like he learned it. That's why I always felt he and I were so different. That's why he seemed so much more of a man."

"Maybe that's because you weren't there to watch him learn when he was young. You only saw the result."

"That is so true." Jeff paused for a moment and then continued while looking up. "Dad never talked about what his life was like when he was young. Like before Mom. He was always so respectful of Mom, he always opened doors for her. He wouldn't sit down at the table until she was there. He never talked about what I needed to hear, like how he handled the thing with girls when he was young. I don't think he was always getting tripped up like me."

"Sure, and we can talk more about this, but it's interesting that with Noel, there doesn't seem to be something that 'tripped you up.' It was your own decision."

"That's true, but it all amounts to the same thing. I never get what I want. Whether it's the girl herself, or somebody else interrupting, or whether it's me and 'what's the right thing to do.' The end result is always the same. Even the code trips me up."

"So instead of being 'grateful' to your code for the guidance it gives you, you feel it stops you from getting what you want?"

Jeff smiled sheepishly. "Yeah, now that you put it that way, that is how I feel." He sighed. "I keep coming back to this. I know I should feel that it makes all the difference when you know you're doing it for yourself." He was shaking his head. "But I'm not there yet."

As the session was coming to a close, Jeff stood and, as he was putting on his coat, he mentioned that his aging mother had finally agreed to move into assisted living and that he would be spending the weekend helping her clean out their family home in Yonkers, just north of the city. He said he was not looking forward to the task since the burden fell on him as the only child. "I hope I'm doing this for myself," he said.

Chapter Four—Michelle

The Office of Dr. Grace Brennan.

Hours By Appointment.

Friday, December 3, 2010.

For her first appointment after the Thanksgiving break, Michelle came just five minutes late. She took off a tiger stripe raincoat and sat down with a huff on the sofa. She was wearing a royal blue dot-jacquard sleeveless dress with a high braided neck and chrome silver heels. It was a stunning look, but the scowl on her face didn't match the outfit. She leaned over the fresh roses I'd placed on a side table and sniffed. Her face softened a bit.

"Last time I didn't tell you something about Mimi," she said.

"What's that?"

"She died."

I waited.

"Someone put poison out for the deer. She ate it. I got home from high school and she was waiting for me on the front porch. She was in her basket where she used to sleep while I read on the rocker. I knew something was wrong when she didn't get up and run to meet me. I dropped my school bag and put her head on my lap. I said I love you, Mimi. She just sighed. And that was it. It was like she waited to die so I could say goodbye."

"I'm so sorry."

"Don't be sorry. I don't want anyone to be sorry for me."

"Ok."

Tears were running down Michelle's cheeks, but her jaw was set.

"Nobody knows all this about me."

"All this?"

"I lost Mimi, but I'm glad for every minute I had with her. I gave my heart to her and she gave hers to me. I didn't hold anything back. To some people, that's just dumb, you can't do that with an animal. But I know different. You can love an animal and they can love you back."

"Yes, we do know you can love."

"I can." Michelle nodded. "Nobody's ever known that about me. Some people think I'm all about being spoiled and cynical. I know why they think it. But they don't know me." She asked in a quiet voice, "Do you think I'm cynical? I want to know what you think."

"I think you've had to deal with some difficult things."

She raised her voice. "So will you get real? Just say it. You think I'm cynical."

I was learning that even the most noncommittal statement of sympathy could set off Michelle's sudden anger. I said, "What does cynical mean to you?"

"There you go again. This can't get me anywhere," she said. "Last time you said there could be something righteous about my complaints. That's bullshit. All I do is complain and complain. There isn't any point to it." She glared at me again. "Is there?"

"Why do you think you need to complain?"

Michelle sighed. "I suppose it's to get relief. On a temporary basis anyway."

"What about on a permanent basis?"

"Permanent? Everyone always says, 'Michelle, there you go again, bitching again.' I just go round and round without getting anywhere."

"I would say then that you need to take these complaints much more seriously. You have to find out what's behind them if you want to have a shot at permanent relief."

"This is very weird, very fucked-up sounding," she said. "You're telling me I don't complain enough?"

"Here, every complaint deserves devoted attention. That's it's 'right,' so to speak. That means you have to follow every complaint all the way to the bottom, and then you have to allow yourself to be changed by your complaints."

"I have no idea what that means."

"If we follow your complaint about being bored, for example, we'll find something very valuable underneath it."

"Like what?"

"I think you're not so much bored as blocked."

"Huh?"

"Something important wants to get through, but it can't yet. We'll have to see what it is."

Michelle laughed. "Ok, fine, I'm up for complaint therapy. I kind of feel flattered. I didn't know my complaints were worth jackshit." Then she screwed up her face. "I'd like to make an official complaint about something. It's something I've never told anybody. I don't like sex. I suppose that makes me weird. Fucked up. My boyfriends are always freaked out by it."

"You tell them?"

"No, I just make excuses. My boyfriends want sex all the time, but I'm just not interested."

"Oh, that sounds difficult."

"Yeah. Do you think there's a connection between my being bored and not liking sex?" she asked.

"Could be," I said. "What might be the connection?"

"You said I'm not so much bored as blocked. Couldn't I be blocked about sex too?"

"Makes sense."

"What would I be blocked about?" Michelle asked as much to herself as to me. "I think I started out on the wrong foot with men."

"What do you mean?"

"My mother says I matured early. My teacher saw some of the boys looking at me in class. When my parents heard about it, they came down really hard on me. So hard it scared me. Like I was going to mess up the whole world. And then it seemed like they were right when I did." Michelle began to cry again.

"What does that mean?"

"The same time that was happening, their nasty neighbor friend was hitting on me and he was married and older than Daddy. Whenever he came over, I'd hide from him in my own house. I'd go in a closet and cry. And my mother says it's the big reason she's disappointed in me."

"Why does she say that?"

"I'll tell you. It all came up again when I was home the other day.

I was there because a women's magazine was interviewing my mother. You know, they do these human-interest stories about the wife of the politician. Lots of fluff about 'our exclusive look inside their most intimate spaces.' They asked for her daughters to be there but my sisters said they were busy. My mother said she called me first, but I doubt it. Anyway, I took the afternoon off from work. My mother knows I don't get paid when I take time off."

I nodded. "So you were doing something you thought she might appreciate?"

"Right. My mother has this sitting room where she entertains business guests. It's got chintz curtains, chintz sofas, everything is flowery chintz, even the wallpaper. It's so overwhelming it could make you gag. My mother and I don't have the same taste. But she is so smart. She was wearing a floor-length red gown to set herself off from all the chintz. I have to say it pretty much worked. It was kind of spellbinding. You couldn't take your eyes off her."

Michelle slipped her feet from her heels, rearranged herself with her feet under her on the sofa and continued with her story.

"The reporter was a woman younger than me. You know, kind of starry-eyed. My mother is always the great hostess. She took the reporter by the elbow and showed off the house. She was all charm and chatty talk, all about 'when the girls were young I loved to dress them alike' and stuff like that. Then a photographer came and they posed a bunch of shots with my mother's arm around my waist, all lovey-dovey. She showed them pictures of the three of us when we were in matching sundresses when I was in grade school. They took the photographs with them when they left. When they were gone, my mother and I were taking the coffee cups into the kitchen and all of a sudden, she laid into me."

"What did she say?"

"She put down the cups, they're chintz too, with a bang, and she said:

"All three of you weren't what I was expecting."

"What were you expecting, Mother?"

"You're all a disappointment to me."

"All of us? Why?"

"I thought you would compete with me the way I did with my mother. But you're all so weak."

"Well, I'm sorry you're so disappointed, Mother. I'm sure it has nothing to do with you."

"Don't get sarcastic with me, Michelle. You know I have very good reasons to be disappointed in you."

At that moment, Michelle stopped her story and seemed to be waiting for me to ask a question and so I asked it.

"What did she mean by that?"

"She's talking about what happened with our neighbor, that guy was who was always hitting on me."

"What does that mean?"

"Back then, I told her he was always cornering me on the stairs and things like that."

"That's why she's disappointed in you?"

"No. Not exactly."

I waited.

Michelle began to cry. "I don't like telling you about this."

Again, I waited.

"You won't like me as much."

"Can I guess that you don't like yourself because of what happened? And you think I might join you in that?"

Michelle smiled through her tears. "You're so smart." She took a tissue from the table and wiped her face.

"Ok, so one time he came over when nobody was home. I was in high school and I was going to a football game. I had on one of those short flare skirts. It was the school colors. He got me on the stairs and he put his hands under my skirt. And then the maid came in the back door and he stopped and left in a hurry. And like a dope, I told my mother about it."

"What did she say?"

"At first she looked really angry. I thought she was angry with him. But then she said:

"You must have done something to give him encouragement."

"I must have?"

"When he put his hands under your skirt, did you let him?"

"I don't know. No. Maybe. I don't know."

"How long?"

"I don't know."

"Then you can't make a fuss about him."

"But that's not fair."

"Fair has nothing to do with it. You're as much to blame as he is."

"Why am I to blame?"

"Don't tell me you didn't like it."

"I didn't, I hated it."

"Then why did you let him?"

"I don't know. I don't know."

"You're just like your sisters."

Michelle wiped her eyes with more tissues from the side table. "I'm crying now just like I did then. My mother doesn't like tears. They just make her mad."

"That was all?"

"No, no. Then she said:

"Michelle, this will be our little secret. Just you and me. You let a disgusting man do things to you. Ok, it's done. He didn't get the message. No one needs to know. We're up for reelection and we don't need any bad press right now. We're not going to talk about this again. I'll make sure it doesn't go on."

Again, Michelle stopped telling her story and I asked, "What did she mean when she said he didn't get the message?"

"I found out later he was doing it to Beth before me."

"She let him go on until he got to you?"

Michelle face grew red.

"Your mother wasn't very protective, was she?"

"No, she wasn't." Michelle started to cry again and then pulled herself together. "So last week, after she said I was disappointing, we were still in the kitchen and I asked her:

"Mother, if you think we're all so weak, why didn't we come out strong like you?"

"Michelle, it's time you did get strong. It's time you grew up about life."

"What do you mean?"

"I mean, you'd better start learning what a woman has to do."

"The way you do it? Your way is best?"

"It's not my way, Michelle, it's the way things are. It's reality."

"It's your reality, isn't that what you mean?"

"It's your reality too."

"You let that reporter think we're all a happy family. Was that reality?"

"It won't hurt you to do your part for this family. It's good press and it's what your father needs to get reelected."

"That's all you care about."

"I care about you, Michelle, and that's why I want you to face reality about your life and about getting a man."

"What do I need to know about getting a man?"

"Michelle, I've told you before that men have to be run by women. They're not princes arriving on a white horse. They're not here to rescue you. If you don't let them know you're running the show, you can make them do what you want. But you have to take charge of them, and you have to be strong."

"But I don't want a man who's a fool. I don't want to run the show."

"Stop being a baby, Michelle. Do you think I got everything I wanted in life? Do you think everything is perfect between your father and me? You've got to stop thinking the world is all about you, Michelle, or you'll be as disappointed as your sisters."

"Maybe you're the one who's so disappointed, Mother."

"Michelle, when you talk like that, I worry about you."

"It's me who worries about you, Mother."

"What? Why on earth would you worry about me?"

"Because you don't get the love you need."

"I do fine just as I am."

"Maybe you do and maybe you don't. Let's leave it there."

Michelle stopped her story. The tears were dry, and she looked tired. "So I didn't want to talk about it anymore with her, but I thought I'd better talk about it with you."

"There's a lot there. What part do you want to talk about?"

"Don't you think I have good reason to be disappointed in myself? Look at how I screwed things up. I let that man touch me. I'll never be able to change that."

"You said you let him?"

"Yeah, I froze."

"You froze?"

"It was like I was in a dream. I couldn't move. I wanted to scream but I couldn't."

"Michelle, that doesn't mean you let him touch you."

"What are you talking about?"

"Freezing is what happens when a person feels they can't run and they can't fight. It's called involuntary paralysis."

"So? Why does that help?"

"Many other women have had to deal with this. You're holding yourself responsible for something you had no choice over."

"That sounds too easy. Aren't you letting me off the hook?"

"Not at all. Freezing is an instinct that takes over, whether we like it or not. What happened was beyond your capacity to do anything else."

"You really think that?"

"I do. You were young and you had no choice. It's not something to carry as a disappointment about yourself all your life."

"Really and truly? You're not just saying it to make me feel better?"

"No."

"So I don't have to feel like my mother's right about me?"

"Now, that is something you do have a choice about."

"But if I'm not disappointed in myself, I don't know who I'll be. I mean, I've always been disappointed in myself. I don't know any other way to be." She sighed several times.

I felt called upon to be very direct. "Michelle, a mother's disappointment in her child is like a curse. And that can last a lifetime. I think your curse is starting to lift."

"What are you talking about?"

"I think you've already begun to realize the disappointment is not entirely about you. It's an inheritance from your mother. You've been carrying her disappointment."

"What do you mean, I'm not disappointed? I feel disappointed. Aren't you being just like those psychiatrists? Aren't you telling me what I feel is wrong?"

"I know you feel that way, but I also think you've taken on your mother's disappointment as if it was your own."

"Why couldn't I be so disappointed all on my own?"

"Because your disappointment has an older person's 'feel' to it. You haven't lived enough of your life, including the part with love, to have accumulated years of profound disappointment. Your mother has."

"You're saying I might not have a love life like hers? And she can't see that?"

"That's very sharp, Michelle. From what you've told me, your mother is disappointed about lots of things in life. It seems to color everything she does. Of course, we know you've had your own painful and difficult things. But overall, most of your story has yet to be written."

"I'm not old enough to be really disappointed in life?"

"Exactly."

"But I feel like she's right about a lot of things." She sighed, looked again at the roses on the side table, and then sighed again. "Ok, maybe my mother's wrong about how I froze, maybe I'm not to blame. That does feel good. But when she says I'm a baby with men, I know she's exactly right."

"If you're too old in one place in your life, you'll be too young in another."

"That's the way it works?"

"Yes."

"So, will I always be too young, inside somewhere?"

"We'll have to see. It may be something you have to carry through life."

"Ugh. You don't spare me, do you?"

I was silent. After a few moments, Michelle broke the silence.

"What does that mean, to carry something?"

"It may be something you will have to account for as your life unfolds."

"Keep track of?"

"Yes."

We paused, and Michelle took a bottle of water from her shopping bag and drank for more than one gulp.

"There's something more about the neighbor."

"What's that?"

"We were at a barbecue in the backyard at another neighbor's house, a few months after that thing happened on the stairs. Everyone was drinking around the pool. There were lots of people there. He came up to me and said he couldn't stop thinking about me, I was haunting his dreams. He asked me to meet him afterward at the park to tell me about it. I didn't say anything, I just walked away, but I went up to this boy in my class who liked me, and I asked him to kiss me hard right in the middle of the party. I wanted the neighbor to see it. I thought he might stop hitting on me. Then my mother saw me making out with this boy who had his hands all over me, and she was convinced I was a slut, and it was definitely me who made the neighbor do what he did."

"So that little scheme backfired on you?"

"Big time."

"That's the way it works, too, isn't it?"

"You got that right. My mother is convinced I'm a sex maniac. She said she saw it with her own eyes. Now nothing will ever convince her otherwise."

Chapter Five—Jeff

The Office of Dr. Yoav Zein. Psychotherapy.

Hours By Appointment.

Friday, December 3, 2010.

Jeff entered our next session with his face flushed, visibly excited, sat quickly, and immediately began recounting the work he'd done at his family home, preparing for his mother's move. In the basement, he moved old lawnmowers, sports equipment, exercise machines that hadn't been used in decades, boxes of hats, card tables and chairs and dusty tarps. Pushing aside a pile of inner tubes and tires, he uncovered a large heavyweight seabag he had never seen before. It was a Navy issue duffel from his father's years as a petty officer.

Jeff leaned forward, speaking nervously, "There were hundreds of letters in the bag. Some were from my Dad to my grandparents, and some were to my Mom, who was his girlfriend then. There were letters back and forth to his brother and sister, and to his friends. I sat there on a tire in the basement and I read this stuff from before I was born. It's amazing how chatty my Dad was."

The letters were full of details about Navy life, regulations, duties, and especially the food. "Chicken on a raft," his father explained to Jeff's mother, was "eggs on toast but not as good as yours, honey." The letters had a cheerful, newsy tone and Jeff found himself smiling at his father's little stories and jokes.

Jeff said he needed to stop reading and get on with the clean-up of the basement, so he took out one final letter to read from the bag. This randomly chosen letter was from his father to his grandfather and was dated just after Jeff's birth. He said the first part of the letter was more news about life in the Navy, but the end of the letter left him in tears. He took this letter out of his shirt pocket, carefully unfolded it, and read it to me:

"I won't be as good a father as you were, Pa. I know that. I just hope my son will be someone I can be proud of. I know I'm not much, and I don't have much to give him, but I can tell him about you. I tried to make you proud, Pa. I hope you know that. Even if I let you down at times, you didn't say anything. Don't think I didn't know what you were thinking. Maybe it's better that way. Your loving son, Don."

This was a side of his father, Jeff said, that he had never seen before. "He did have his doubts. Even about being a father." Jeff shook his head back and forth. "This is just like what happened with Mike and Noel."

"What's the connection?"

"Nothing was what it seemed with them. And now nothing is like what it seemed with my Dad. Everything in my life isn't what it seemed. It's like I was living my life upside down. Now I'm standing right side up and I'm dizzy."

For the rest of this session, Jeff filled out the portrait of his father that was revealed in the letters. His father was now a man with thoughts and feelings, however unexpressed to Jeff.

"It's so weird. I have these moments when I look at my father like he was a different person. Then I go back to the way I saw him before I found the letters. Then I switch back again. I do it with Mike and Noel too. It's like flipping a coin, only I have a choice on which side it lands." He added, "But there's one thing I can't flip."

I waited silently as he opened his briefcase, took out a photograph, and handed it to me.

"I found this in the duffel bag. It's Dad and Mom, and me in the middle. It was on a fishing trip when I was eight. When I look at it, I feel so sad."

"About?"

"I feel like it was all a misunderstanding. My father kept his distance because he thought he didn't have much to offer me as a Dad. I thought he was more of a man than I was and kept my distance because I thought I didn't measure up to him. It was all a mistake. I wish I could have him back and tell him…tell him…"

"Tell him what?"

"I don't know. I don't know. It's so hard. I feel like the chance to talk to him got taken from me. It's past and I can't get it back. It's one of those things I can't flip the coin on."

"Now if you had the chance, what would you say?"

"I don't know. Maybe I'm not any better at finding the words than he was. All I know is he wasn't the person I thought he was, and I'm not the person I thought I was."

There was a long silence, and then the session came to an end with Jeff sighing several times. The thoughts and feelings we had opened up were left hanging, unresolved.

The sessions that followed in the winter weeks were filled with rehashing much of what he had already said. There were lengthy descriptions of frustrating sex episodes from the past, there were moments from fishing trips during childhood with his father when Jeff wanted to ask questions but held to silence, and there were daydreams about women, women he was not dating. In each session, the themes of Jeff's life were woven back and forth into a tapestry of events, thoughts, and desires. Frustration, Jeff said, was the unifying thread.

On a beautiful but still chilly spring day in early April, winter finally seemed to have lost its grip. Jeff came into the office, took off a lightweight dark blue down jacket, sat down, stared at me with raised eyebrows and said again, "I don't know, I don't know." His glance fell on a bunch of daffodils on the glass table. In Central Park, the daffodils and the grape hyacinth were in full bloom, and the forsythia was about to burst out in full yellow glory. Jeff picked at the button on his shirt cuff. "I don't know. There were so many things I didn't tell my Dad. Even some things I didn't tell you."

I was silent.

"There's one thing I didn't tell you before, but I want to now. It's about Mike. Remember the first time I came here, you said the important events in life can reflect things back to us? Things we need to know about ourselves?"

"Yes, I remember."

"Well, it must be true about the important people too, right?"

"For sure."

"So I need to know things about myself and Mike before I can go on with my life. Things he did sometimes seem like things that happened to me. Is that weird?"

"I think that can happen when the boundaries between you and another person are blurred and aren't well-drawn. Their experiences can seem to be your experiences."

"Yeah, that's why I want to tell you about what happened."

Jeff said the arrival of spring brought back to mind a story about Mike, a story that haunted Jeff. When they were still in the first year of college, Mike left school by himself for a trip south during the height of spring break. Mike went to Florida for a specific reason. He had heard about a large drunken orgy that regularly took place in a completely dark room. With his usual determination, he found the party on his first night. In the darkness, Mike groped around for a female torso and ejaculated into a woman he was never to set eyes on, a woman whose face he never did see. When he returned to the dorm after spring break, he told the story to the others with much laughter and joking all around. The others joked about the fact that Mike had no idea if this union had resulted in a child. The idea of Mike as an anonymous father was the source of a great deal of amusement among the boys. They created several scenarios involving detectives and DNA in which a child or a teenager might appear in Mike's later life and start calling him "Dad." They teased Mike about needing to keep an extra room wherever he went in case the "son" showed up and asked to move in. Jeff found himself listening uneasily to the conversation.

"Everybody was saying about how he might have gotten AIDS and stuff," Jeff said. "But that's not what I found myself thinking about."

"What were you thinking about?"

"It all seems so dead end."

"Can you say what it is that's dead end?"

"This thing about scoring, doing it with somebody you'll never meet. It's so much like Mike. To the core. It just seems like it doesn't go anywhere, it's a dead end. I mean, where do you go from there in life? Do you just do the same thing all over again?"

"Good question."

"I don't know, but like I said, this thing about Florida keeps coming back to me. Like I said, it haunts me. What was Mike really doing there?"

"And what does it have to do with you?"

"Okay. Right. I have no idea. What do you think?"

"You said Mike gets upset if he has to drink alone?"

"He does. Why do you ask that?"

"He doesn't have much of a way of connecting with other people, does he?"

"That's exactly right. It's usually him and the people at a bar."

"What if we see this episode from a different angle? What if Mike was doing his best to connect with other people, especially women?"

"Doing his best, but completely in the dark?"

"I think that's right."

"Oh, that's awful." Again Jeff was thinking hard. "I guess it must have bothered me so much because I was in the dark too. I mean with women."

"That's a powerful realization, Jeff."

"Yeah, we were both doing the best we could. But it wasn't getting us anywhere."

"Yes, that's a really stark conclusion, isn't it?"

"That is really sad. God, it's pathetic." Jeff looked pained. "This is really hard to take in. As messed up as it sounds, he was trying to do something positive for himself when he went down to Florida?"

"I think so. When you peel away the layers underneath most negative behavior, at bottom there's usually something positive that's trying to get expressed."

"Only it came out really screwed up?"

"Yes."

"You know I just saw something I never saw before. When Mike was in that dark room, it wasn't just the women nobody could see. It was Mike too, like he was invisible. It's like he wasn't there as far as anybody else was concerned. He was nobody to anybody. That must be really alienating, right?"

"Oh, yes."

"Now I think I know why this Florida thing came back to me over and over again. I don't want to be nobody to anybody. It's a horrible feeling and I think I've been dodging it for a long time." Jeff was holding his sides again. "That must be why I needed to tell you about Mike. We're both people who go around feeling like we're living life in the dark."

Once again, we let those words hang in the air for long moments. Finally, Jeff said, "I feel like I should flip it with Mike too."

"What does that mean?"

"Flip how I see him, like I'm doing with my Dad. Maybe there's something positive about Mike that I didn't know about?"

"Ok, what could that be?"

"Everybody says he's a doer."

"He goes after what he wants?"

"Yeah, I think that's it."

"So how are you at going after what you want?"

"Not as determined." He looked dejected.

"You'd like his capacity for pursuit, but for goals that are more in keeping with what's right for you?"

"That's good. And what about Mike? Does it make sense to ask? What was he in the friendship for, with me?"

"What's your idea?"

"I don't have one."

"You said Mike told you he went for Noel because you thought she was hot."

"Yeah. Do you really think he was looking to me to find out what to go for?"

"Yes, I think you can take him at his word. He thought you knew what was valuable."

"Oh no, I'm sorry I led him into that," Jeff said. "A bad marriage."

"Of course, it's his responsibility. But it is interesting you used that phrase. What you 'led him into.' I've had the impression that you thought Mike was leading things all the time in your friendship."

"You're right, I did." Jeff was blinking hard. "We had this thing going, I guess. He was like the brother I never had. Now that I look back on it, I can see that I must have influenced him too. I'm really sorry I had no idea what kind of a woman to go for, and neither did he."

We let this idea sink in. After a few moments, he said, "There were others he could have picked up on. From me." Jeff then described another woman, Jo, who also later became the wife of one of his college friends. Jeff had also been "turned on" by Jo for years before her marriage. "Do you think it means something?" he asked. "That I had these two things for Noel and Jo?"

"I think it's time to face something difficult. It seems the only women you've seen yourself as capable of being involved with are your friends' wives," I said. "You haven't seen yourself as meriting a mate of your own."

"God, that sounds awful," Jeff said. His mouth was open and he was shaking his head. "I guess I really haven't thought much of myself." The noise of the traffic outside the open window filled the room. We both seemed to be listening to it and to the echo of Jeff's statement. The session seemed to be reaching for a conclusive moment.

"What you think of yourself really determines what kind of woman you go for?"

"How could it be otherwise?"

Jeff looked down, then pulled out a tissue from the box and dabbed his eyes.

"This all makes me think maybe there was another reason I didn't do it with Noel."

"What was that?"

"I wasn't sure she was in the sleeping bag for me."

"Go on."

"I kind of knew she was there to give Mike some payback for screwing around. She was using me to get back at him. I felt like I was a pawn in her game."

"That's sobering, isn't it?"

Jeff sighed. "I've got to learn it's no good unless the woman is really there for me." With that, he stopped dabbing his eyes, looked up and clenched the tissue in his fist.

"I think I missed out on the advice my Dad could have given me about women. I really wish we could've talked about it. It's another place where the chance to talk to him got taken away from me."

"May I push a little here?"

"Sure."

"Let's try again. What would you want to say to him if you could speak to him now?"

"I still don't know."

"I think you'd want a father and son moment with him."

Jeff burst into tears and sobbed. With his chest heaving and his voice choking, he said, "I would. We never really had that, I mean where we really talked."

"And if you did?"

"I wouldn't know what else to tell him except I love him. I love you, Dad." He wiped his face with the tissue. Sobbing again, he said, "He probably wouldn't be able to say anything back, so I'd tell him I know he loves me."

I was silent.

"I know you love me, Dad."

With that, the sobbing stopped and Jeff wiped his face again. "Wow, that was something," he said. "I didn't know I could that."

Chapter Six—Michelle
The Office of Dr. Grace Brennan.
Hours By Appointment.

Friday, April 29, 2011.

In a session on a gloriously bright and warm day at the end of April, Michelle was again stunningly dressed. She wore a beige sleeveless open-knit dress with a straight silhouette and an elegant ribbed neckline. Her heels were matching beige, with crisscrossed straps over the ankle. She struck a pose like a model. "Do you like it?" she asked.

"It's a work of art," I said.

"Yeah," she sighed. "You could wear this too, couldn't you?"

As we both smiled, I noted to myself this comment was an important moment in building something people have called the therapeutic alliance. After our rocky start, the reasonable side of each of us was operating in tandem, producing a kind of harmony that came from working together toward a goal. It was all very fine, but of course it could only go so far uninterrupted.

"I know it looks good," she said, "but why do we it? Why do I do it? I really don't think I do it for men. I think they're all crazy."

"I see."

"I suppose you don't think so. Maybe you've had it better. I hope you have."

I was silent.

"For me, that's all I know about men. You said I'm carrying my mother's disappointments? Shouldn't we be talking about my own disappointments?"

"Fair enough."

"Well, men are definitely my own disappointments. One thing I've learned is men don't care about you, they don't even know you're there half the time."

"That's been your experience."

"You keep saying that. Believe me, it's always been that way."

"I see."

"Men don't have sex with you, they have sex at you. I got the biggest dose of that in college."

"What happened in college?"

"I hooked up with this guy Tom when I was a freshman. It was my first time. We got into bed and he just jumped on me and it hurt and it was over in a minute. Afterward, he stood up and did stretches and then he went to the bathroom and read a sports magazine in there for a long time. I was just sunk, lying there in the bed, feeling incredibly alone. Then later he wanted it over and over, like I was his personal milking machine. I started dreading it, so I got good at making excuses. I thought it might just be like that with him, but it's been like that with everyone else."

"Perhaps you haven't had the right partner," I said.

"What do you mean?"

"Sex may only be good for you with the right partner. That's true for a surprising number of women."

"Why should that make it any different?"

"When it goes right, sex should make the woman feel more like a woman. I don't think you've had that experience yet."

"That's true," she said ruefully. "I just feel sweaty and disgusted afterward." She paused. "So what does `more like a woman' feel like?"

"What would you say?"

"I haven't the faintest idea. I only know what `less like a woman' feels like."

Michelle seemed thoughtful. Then, throwing her head back and hooting with laughter, she said: "So I have to find somebody who isn't a grunter." Laughing helplessly at her own joke, Michelle lay back in the sofa and wiped away tears. "You don't seem to think it's funny." She stared at me.

"What's this about grunting?"

Michelle said that during sex, her boyfriends were passionately engaged, grunting with self-absorbed effort and pleasure, while she "observed" the process and found herself bored on the one hand, and enraged at their indifference to her on the other. Afterward, she often felt the urge to flee.

I took this moment as the opportunity to reflect back to her what she had been saying in this session and in our previous sessions. "There does seem to be a connection in the way you describe your experience of sex and other things in life, like work," I said. "Everybody else is grunting from effort or pleasure while ignoring you, and you're watching the whole thing, bored or fighting the urge to run away.'"

Michelle sat up. "That's right," she said. She looked thoughtful and asked, "What's the opposite of a guy who ignores you?"

"Good question."

"I really don't know. He would have to be a Prince." She hesitated for a long moment. "You won't laugh at me?"

"Laugh at you?"

"Ok, ok, I've never told anybody ever, ever."

I nodded.

"I want to be held."

I nodded again.

"I want a Prince to hold me."

"Yes?"

For the first time, Michelle had something positive to say about men in front of me. It was a significant development, a breakthrough. She looked up at the ceiling. Out came a flood of words filled with longing. Michelle had secret daydreams of a man who was enamored with her. He was princely and he cared deeply for her. "It's so romantic. It happens some nights when I'm in bed. I think of him. He comes to me and says he can't live without me. I'm his inspiration."

Michelle looked down and saw me. She put on her "drop dead" look and said, "You have no right to judge me."

"Judge you?"

"I can see it on your face. You're looking down on me just like my mother. You think I'm a baby." Then she wept. After a long silence, she said, "I'm sorry, I don't think you're judging me. I'm judging myself. I guess I am a big baby."

"Michelle, don't you think every young girl has the right to have fantasies about love and romance?"

"Yes, but not at my age."

"I think your dreams of how love could be were prematurely curtailed."

"You mean my nasty neighbor and how my Mother blamed me?"

"Yes, that and more. It seems the tender side of love was blocked at the door in your home."

"That's for sure."

"And so something difficult came in through the window."

"What was that?"

"The harsh side of sex."

"Harsh? I guess that's what did happen with Tom." Michelle looked at me, searching my face. "You won't laugh at me?"

Once again, I was silent.

"I was scared that first time, but I was really more excited. I'd always thought that your first time was when a great love might come into your life. I really did believe what they told me, how my virginity was a gift to a man. I was sure Tom would appreciate what a special bond it would mean for us. I even had fantasies of having his child, but at least I knew enough not to do that. So I asked Tom if he would wear a condom. He said, 'No. That's your business, not mine,' so I went on the pill."

"I see."

"He used to wake me up from a sound sleep for sex, and if I wasn't up for it, he got really angry. One time when I was really tired and didn't want to, he grabbed me by the shoulders and shook me, and he said, 'you look like you're sexy, but you're not.' That just hurt like hell and I cried and he apologized and he even cried himself. Then he jammed himself into me, it was over in a minute, and then he fell asleep."

With experiences of criticism like that, I thought, it was no wonder Michelle could compare sex to the cold workings of a machine. She asked her question again. "So what else is there to sex besides feeling less like a woman?"

"What do you think?"

"You tell me. You're the expert." There was sarcasm in her voice. "Or at least I hope you are." She added, "Oh, I suppose you're going to tell me there's something noble about sex."

"If it goes right, it's meant to be uplifting."

"Is that really true?"

"Very much so."

Michelle suddenly was very upset. "Oh, God, oh my God, what am I doing?" she said.

I waited for her to continue.

"Here I am hoping for a man to come along who'll love me and I'm not even sure he exists. I'm holding out for something nobody believes in. Nobody but you." The words seemed to choke her. Tears ran down her face. "I want that. I want to be lifted up. How can I know if it's meant to be? What if I'm fooling myself?" She looked at me with a most imploring expression. "Please don't bullshit me. Do you think it's meant to be, for me?"

"I don't know the future for anyone," I said, "but I don't see any reason why it wouldn't be meant for you. I think you should act as if love is meant for you."

"Why do you say that?"

"Because love is always a possibility for human beings. It's all around us, and we have to do our best to let it come into our lives."

Michelle dried her tears with a Kleenex. "So then it's my fault if it wasn't uplifting? I wasn't letting love come into my life?"

"Again, I don't think you've had the right partner. Beyond a certain point, it isn't really productive to think of it as your fault."

"That's not what the men think. Tom said I was hung up about sex. I thought it was a line, but I guess I bought into what he said. And every other boyfriend since has said the same thing. I thought maybe it was my fault for wanting a prince."

"For now let's stick with what you told me, with what you experienced. I can't imagine sex would be very much fun with someone who was regularly criticizing you."

"You're not just being nice to me?"

"Is that the way you've experienced me?"

"No, you don't let me get away with anything." Michelle sighed. "If I listened to you about this, I'd take a big load off my shoulders, wouldn't I?"

"You would, yes."

"I can't believe it. You're the only one who doesn't always want to come down on me and tell me it's all my fault."

"Yes, and since you know that, let's move on, and start talking about men and love and sex in a new way."

"What do you mean?"

"You've been with men who were fault-finders, and we know you you've found a lot of fault with yourself and with them. It's important to keep all of that in mind. There was plenty of blame to go around and there's no point in ignoring all of that. But at the same time, there's also a way of looking at things that doesn't involve finding fault."

"What's that?"

"I think you weren't ready for sex and love. And it sounds like your boyfriends weren't either. That's a just-so fact."

"I have no idea what that means."

"As I said, it's a new way of thinking about things. We'll have to talk a lot more about it, but I think it's the most important fact about you."

"Not my fault? Not ready?"

"Right."

"With you, I never get what you're saying right away." She gave a small smile. "But sometimes later, it makes sense." She added, "I think you're telling me there's a way of letting go of everybody fighting to prove someone else is wrong. Is that it?"

"Michelle, you went right for the bottom line."

We had reached the end of the session and I stood up, but for once Michelle continued to sit. Then she stood up so suddenly that she seemed to bounce off the sofa and said, "This is amazing. Everybody I know finds fault with everybody. It's what everybody's doing all the time, it's one big screaming mess. Now you're telling me about a different world, but I don't know anything about it." Still standing, she didn't move to the door. "Do other people really live in that world? Do you really live in that world?" she asked. "For real?"

Once again, I thought of the therapeutic alliance, and how so much of the benefit of therapy comes from the shared experience of both partners doing the work together. In taking a chance to trust me and my experience, I knew she was looking past me, for a way to find her trust in herself. Then we both moved to the door and I said, "Yes Michelle, that is the world I live in."

Chapter Seven—Jeff

The Office of Dr. Yoav Zein. Psychotherapy.

Hours By Appointment.

Friday, October 28, 2011.

Once again, it was a cool, crisp day in October, an anniversary for Jeff, a full year since our first session. When I opened the door to the office for him, I reminded myself to look with fresh eyes at how he was doing. What, if any, progress had Jeff made? What would be a reliable sign that his life was getting better?

As he sat down on the sofa, he said, "I want to talk about something that happened when I was in my second year at Columbia. It's another one of those things that's been waiting for me to look at, to figure out what happened. There was this girl named Lucia," he began. "She's another piece in the puzzle for me about sex and women."

I waited for him to continue.

"So this happened when I was going out with a girl named Kate, she was a sophomore too. I liked her but it wasn't serious. There was nothing very exciting happening between us. It was a Saturday night and Kate was in her room with a cold, but there was this party we'd planned to go to, and she said I should go ahead, go to the party and have fun. I said, are you sure? She said of course, so I went alone. It was in another hall, and this amazing thing happened when I got there. Lucia was there, I'd seen her before. She was a senior and the hottest girl on campus. It wasn't even right to call her a girl. She looked like she was already a woman. I was staring at her at the party—heavy eye make-up and wavy hair, and a fancy strapless dress. All the girls from my class were wearing jeans and men's shirts and she really stood out. The party was in the hall lounge and the room was crowded, but I pushed through and saw her dancing barefoot. I started dancing in front of her. She didn't seem to have a date. So we were dancing and I thought 'why not be bold? What have you got to lose?' I put my hands on her hips and moved her around the floor. I wondered, does she love this as much as I do? Then she threw both her hands around my neck, and I thought, she does love it. She was swaying in front of me and it seemed like she was ready to do whatever I wanted. I was on fire for her."

Jeff paused for a long moment and seemed caught once again in his memories. I shook him out of his reverie: "What happened then?"

"So we were dancing and I lost track of time. It was so great. Then my mind started racing. Did Lucia have a roommate and, if not, how could I steer her from the dance floor to her room? What if I had to take her back to my room? Would my roommates be there?

"Then my phone vibrated. I took out the phone and then Lucia put both of her hands into my back pockets. She was pulling me closer to her, and she kept dancing. It was like she was hooked onto me. I looked over her shoulder at the phone and saw it was a text from Kate. I thought, I'm not going to answer it, so I put the phone back in my front pocket. Lucia gave me this big wide-eyed look and then she turned around, put her backside into me, and wrapped my arms around her waist. We were dancing front to back. It was amazing. I'd never felt anything like this before.

"I was thinking where can I find a place to be alone with her, and then the phone went off again. Crap. All right, I thought, what is it? I took the phone and put it on Lucia's back. It was Kate again, asking me to pick up some flu medicine and bring it to her room. She was feeling worse.

"I put the phone away and Lucia took my hands in hers and started moving my hands over her stomach in circles. I was in another world. Her belly was so flat and smooth and the music was going with some kind of Latin beat. She turned her head around and smiled at me. That smile was like the sun lighting up the room. Then the music shifted to another song and I got another text. 'R U there?'"

"Kate?" I asked.

Jeff grimaced. "It was so annoying. I wanted to heave the phone out the window. But then I thought, all right, enough is enough. I told Lucia to wait for me, I'd be right back. I went out into the hall and called Kate. She begged me to come with the medicine. She said all her roommates were out and there was no one else she could ask. I told her I would have to get back to her in a little while, I was busy with something. 'Will you call me when you're done?' she asked. I said, 'Sure. I will.'"

Jeff looked at me. "Are you wondering if I meant it?"

"Yes, I think I was."

"Really at that moment I wasn't sure. I was in the hallway and about to run back into the party and I stopped to think. Lucia was the most desirable woman I'd ever been close to, and I could still smell her breath. She'd had a lot of alcohol but her breath was still sweet. I thought to myself, her breath is warm, and her belly is warm. So why wasn't I running back into the party? Kate was nice, but there was no magnetism with her, no magic. She was more like a sister than a girlfriend. She could wait for the medicine. Anyway, I thought, she doesn't really want the medicine, she wants me. But I didn't really want her. Then I made up my mind. I had to know what sex would be like with Lucia. So I charged back to the party. I had to push my way past the people hanging out in the hallway. That seemed to take forever. Then, when I finally got back in, I couldn't find Lucia. The room was dark and really crowded. There were these clumps of people dancing and I had to move around all of them. No Lucia. I thought, there's no way she could have gone home. I went to get a glass of sangria, and drank half of it down, and turned back around to the dancing and I saw Lucia not far away. She was in that same pose, back to front, with the hands of another guy on her stomach. She saw me and she gave me that big wide-eyed look again and a smile.

"I had a flash of anger, and I cursed out loud, and then I started laughing at myself. 'I'm such a dummy,' I thought. 'Of course she's doing it with whoever's there. What else would a girl like her do? Jeff you dope, what makes you think you're the one who's so special?'

"So I finished my drink and I left. I stopped at the drugstore and got the medicine. I was sure Kate would want to take it and talk for hours and be comforted and all that. When I got there, she was asleep."

Like the scenes from many of the other stories he told me, Jeff said this one came back to him over and over again, especially at night. "It's always a struggle," he said. "Women seem to come into my life with a promise. I get hot for them. And then the promise evaporates."

"They're alluring."

"Yeah, I've got a big alluring thing going on. It's a mystery, and it's a big part of the struggle in my life. Why do you think I'm always stopped?" He added, "I would answer this for myself if I could."

He had raised this question many times, and we'd discussed it many times, but so far we hadn't reached the point where anything was satisfying to Jeff. I did trust though that something important and valuable would appear when the moment was right.

"What am I trying to get from these women? All these fantasies, all these women I thought I wanted so much?"

"A very good question. Where would you start?"

"They're very hot."

"You've said that."

"Right. And I think what I'm trying to get is hotness."

"You've never used that word before. Hotness. Can you say more?"

"If I got the woman, I'd feel like my life was so good. I'd be living with hotness, right in my hands. When I was rubbing Lucia's belly while we were dancing, I could feel that hotness in my hands, and it was like I was ready for the same thing in my hands with Noel in the sleeping bag, only both times my hands came up empty."

"But you felt you were close to what you wanted?"

"I did. But then why did I leave Lucia and talk on the phone with Kate? Why do I push away what I want, just when it's about to be mine?"

As we often did, we let his words hang in the air for some moments while Jeff seemed to be collecting his thoughts, digesting what he had just said. Finally, he resumed speaking.

"I think maybe a part of me has always doubted I could get that feeling from a woman, from another person, like someone else couldn't do that for me permanently. But I kept trying anyway, looking for what I need from one special woman, despite the part of me in the back of my head, doubting I could get what I need in life from a woman alone. So of course I had to have the thing with women not work out." Jeff sighed as he said, "I know I'm not the only one."

"What do you mean?"

"I think Mike's always been looking for the same thing, just in his own way. He's always going for something good, with all his women, and he always comes up short, he's never satisfied. It must be why he was so angry with Noel. She was one more failure, but that one really zapped him. For a long time I was wondering why he was in such a rage against her."

"You see some overlap with yourself and Mike?"

"I do. I think he's got the same doubt like me, he's disappointed he can't get what he needs in life from a woman. He's bitter and he blames it on the women. He thinks they've got it, whatever it is, but they're just holding it back from him, just to be bitchy. The last time we talked, he said he thinks women are an illusion, a big nasty joke our minds work on us. He said women are a trick life plays on us."

"That's a very difficult place to be stuck in, isn't it?"

"Oh yeah. He's got things upside down, just like I did. But in his own way of course. He's frustrated about this alluring thing just like I am."

"Don't you think there's a place in life for what you call hotness?" I asked.

"There must be," Jeff said. I was surprised he agreed so readily.

"From everything we've talked about here," he continued, "I'm sure there must be a way women and life could be alluring and it would be ok. The thing is, I've got to be hot for my own life. For a person coming from where I started, that's one hell of a stretch."

"Hot for life. Jeff, I really like that."

"I'm glad you like it."

I noticed that Jeff's scratching at the stubble of his face had lessened, as if his scratching at the old memories for their meaning had produced some results. Now he was rubbing his hands together, as if he was expecting something good to happen next. "I think that's the main message," he said.

"The main message?"

"You know, the message is to get on with the main business of my life, make it good, whatever that is. Get my hands into it. And don't get distracted. There will be alluring things that aren't real and they can sidetrack you if you let them. Even things that might seem really exciting, like making it with Noel. Underneath all the frustration there might be something in me that was aiming at something good. You once said it was a higher power."

"Actually it was you who said that. Is that how you see it now?"

"Yeah, I do. Everything that looks alluring isn't necessarily something you want to run after. If I didn't know that, if I didn't really, really know that, and it's true that I didn't, then something had to step in and stop me. I was in danger of going after things that weren't right for me but I didn't even know it. I might have missed out on the things I was really meant for, so I had to be stopped."

"I think that's very profound."

"The things that stopped me weren't really my enemy, right?"

"Again, Jeff, I find that very profound."

"Thanks. With women, everything happened the way it did, all the frustration, it was because I really needed to go after the main business about being hot for life."

I felt we had just run a marathon in this session. These last few exchanges wrapped up thoughts and feelings that we were working on all year long, and the moment when they coalesced was breathtaking. But Jeff wasn't finished, there was more.

"You can't get the feeling of being alive from women," Jeff said. "Not if you need to get it for yourself. But just maybe, if I can really learn to be in my own life, then I might be ready to go after a woman in the right way, and then nothing would need to stop me."

I couldn't help but expel a deep breath when he said this. The session had reached an end. As if on a high note, at the door Jeff said cheerily, "See you next week."

As might be expected, the mood didn't last. At the start of the next session, Jeff's shoulders were slumped, and he was again shaking his head.

"I didn't tell you something. These 'upside down misunderstandings' in my life," he said, "they're everywhere. Now they're even at my work."

After this comment, I expected to hear of some unpleasant developments. "What's going on at work?"

"You know I've always prided myself about being conscientious at work. Part of my code I guess. Ok, maybe I was even creative once in a while, but most of the time I've been sure I'm expendable. Maybe even invisible. I was trying not to fool myself, so I didn't give myself the luxury of thinking I would last on this job. I've been down on myself for not getting off my behind to look for something else."

"What happened?'

"They announced the annual promotions. They tell me I'm being moved into a job involving corporate strategy for all the magazines of the company. A senior manager told me, 'We have plans for you at this company.' The promotion comes with a really decent raise. I can look for a bigger apartment and sign a lease. Looking back, I don't think there's a single place in my life where I saw things clearly," he finished, shaking his head.

Since I had been expecting bad news, I was taken aback for a moment. Then, once again, I chose to lead Jeff into appraising the present. "Look here Jeff, you're taking this success in the same way you took what you thought were failures."

"What do you mean?"

"I can see you weren't expecting this good thing to happen, but in fact, it did. Isn't that a cause for celebration? Not just another cause for self-criticism?"

Jeff ran his hands through his hair. "Oh, what a mess. You're right, you're right. I guess I've been so caught up in what's gone wrong that I wasn't ready for good things to happen."

"Yes. And we know that's a warning signal for you."

"It is?"

"Here we see an ongoing pattern of yours in operation. A pattern that needs to be stopped. A pattern that can be stopped."

"What pattern are you talking about?"

"Taking even good news as a reason to feel down about yourself."

"It's funny that you said that word. A 'warning.' Right after they called me in to give me the promotion, I felt like a big alarm was going off in my head. I could hear my Dad's voice saying don't trust anything that isn't a struggle. His message was always, 'Watch out! Watch out! Something could be coming!'"

"You can't trust there will be good things?"

"Right. He once said to me 'boy, it's ok to take a break to go fishing, but don't you dare let it go to your head.' For him, everything except a break for fishing, everything in the rest of life, was always going to be a struggle against the odds. That's how it is, and that's how it's always going to be. He thought that was how it would be for me too. I see now he was trying to help me when he gave me the message not to fool myself. Like, don't let yourself get a nasty surprise because life will whack you when you least expect it. And then, of course, I did get lots of nasty surprises, especially with women and sex. So it seemed he was right."

"But now you're wondering again if your father's view of life is right for you?"

"Yeah, I feel weird about it."

"How so?"

"Now, with this promotion, life doesn't have to feel like such a struggle to me. I think I always felt the world is pretty much a hostile place, and now I've got to be open to the fact I might be proved wrong about that, like you say, there's a place for the good things. My Dad wouldn't want me to trust a feeling like that. Aren't I going against him in some way?"

"You're betraying your father's code?"

"Yeah, exactly. It's like my Dad, wherever he is, is angry with me. Really angry. Knowing him, he'll stay angry too."

As the session came to a close, Jeff stood up, shook his head back and forth, and said, "Even with everything that happened, I always loved my dad so much. Even now, I don't want him always to be a father who never knew what it was like to be connected to his son. I don't know why, but I still feel like it's in my power to do something about that. I hope that's not crazy."

Chapter Eight—Michelle
The Office of Dr. Grace Brennan.
Hours By Appointment.

Friday, April 27, 2012.

On this gorgeous but still chilly spring day, Michelle wore a lemon and black wool bouclé jacket with black trim on the pockets and the sleeves. It was a classic vintage look, straight out of the late 1950s, but I knew it was again the height of fashion. As she settled on the couch, she seemed eager and excited.

"I figured something out," she said. "You know how lots of people tell women to accept themselves without a man? It never works when they say that and I finally know why."

"Why is that?" I asked.

"See, nobody ever says what acceptance really is or how you get it, everyone thinks you can just say that to people and that's all there is to it, like you just snap your fingers and boom, you accept yourself. Wouldn't everybody do it if it was that simple?"

"Of course."

"I think lots of women are like me, they think there's something wrong with them if they can't accept themselves, something that's supposed to be so easy."

"I think you're on to something."

"So ok, it's actually really hard to stop focusing your whole life on getting a man. But what else do you focus on? What do you think it is?"

"I would say it's the fulfillment of who we are, in our essence."

"Yeah, that is what you would say," Michelle said, then she looked at me as if for the first time. "I like you," she said.

"And I like you."

She looked satisfied for a moment, but then her face clouded. "I've never said that to anyone before," she said.

As I wondered if this moment of closeness was too much for her, she said, "I wanted you to like me but I wasn't going to pay a price for it. It had to be on my terms or not at all."

"Sure."

"The weirdest thing is, I don't worry anymore about what your terms are. You're not like anybody I've ever known. There's never a price for liking you." With that, as she did so many times, Michelle changed the subject. "You know, I haven't been dating anyone for months now."

"I noticed."

"I don't really know why. Maybe I'm changing too fast to know what I want from a date." She took off the jacket, folded it, and put it across the arm of the sofa. "What you said a moment ago? I have no idea what fulfilling my essence means. It's just words to me. Can't you do better than that?" She glared at me, but then her face softened. "I'm sorry. I'm really sorry. I know I don't need to get all pissy, at

least not with you. But what if I don't ever find anybody? What if I
spend my life looking for a man and I never find him? What if there's
nobody out there, nobody like that sweet and tender kind of guy you
were talking about last time, where you love each other without
always finding fault? What if there's nobody like that out there for
me?"

I was silent.

"You're not reassuring me, are you?" Michelle ran her hands
through her hair. She sat up straight and tears began to pour out of her
eyes.

"God, it could happen. It could really happen. I might be single all
my life." She became so agitated that her hands began to shake. "I
can't accept that. I just can't accept that," she said.

"I think we should talk about what it means to accept something."

Michelle ignored what I said as her face took on the familiar set of
anger I had come to know so well.

"In my twenties I said: Screw men, who needs them, anyway?
They're a bunch of users." She stopped crying and her hands stopped
trembling. "But it was a lie, I never stopped wanting a man. I'm more
honest about it now. That's why I can't accept the idea of being single.
I can't do it."

"Then we have to talk about what acceptance means to you."

She looked up through the last of her tears. "All right, I give in.
Why does acceptance matter so much?"

"If acceptance is genuine, it means you don't have to live with
resignation and bitterness. At their worst, those can last a lifetime."

"I can avoid that?"

"Sure."

"How do you know?"

"Unlike some people, you're not stuck in an immovable place."

After a few moments Michelle slipped off her heels, rubbed her feet, and then curled her feet under the side of the sofa cushion. "Ok, ok, I want to hear more about the right kind of acceptance. I know I have to accept myself more, whatever that means. Why is it so damned difficult?"

"Perhaps because you've swallowed the idea that you would accept yourself, but only conditionally."

"What do you mean, conditionally?"

"On the condition of finding a mate. As you've had plenty of opportunity to see, and not just with your sister Beth, life is often very cruel to those who try to accept themselves conditionally."

"I'm so confused. I thought holding out for a man to make me happy would keep me from being bitter." Michelle sighed in puzzlement. "The only place I ever got acceptance was from Mimi. And now from you. I know you accept me. But I don't know how. I wish I could accept myself like you do." Picking up her head, she asked, "How do you do it?"

"I accept you and everything you bring here with interest and curiosity and an eye toward exploration."

Michelle sat up straight. "You mean that's what acceptance is?"

"Yes."

"I thought it was something colossal. Like Gandhi or Mother Theresa. I thought I'd have to become a fucking saint or something." She was clearly thinking hard. "So that means I don't have to give up on the idea of getting a mate?"

"Who said you should?"

"Wait a minute, I thought you said so."

"We've been talking about accepting yourself as you are, without a mate. You can live a very good and fulfilling life without a mate. You have that capability. But that doesn't mean you have to give up wanting a partner."

"Oh, my God, that's so simple. Why didn't I get it before?"

"Maybe it's not so simple."

Michelle rearranged her feet on the opposite side of the sofa and arched her shoulders back.

"I don't want to accept something about me," she said.

"Yes?"

"You remember Tom, the first guy I was with?"

"Yes I do."

"I was in bed with him, lying in his arms, it was so peaceful and quiet, and he said, 'You know Michelle, you're a big baby.'"

"Oh my."

"Yeah, it just sliced through me. I was so shaken up. I ran into the bathroom and I cried for an hour. When I came out, he'd gone."

"Oh dear."

"Yeah, so for a long time, I accepted he was right. And I accepted there was nothing I could do about it."

"And now?"

"I'm not so sure."

Michelle refolded the bouclé jacket and laid it carefully over the arm of the sofa. "There's something I'm scared to ask."

I waited.

"I want to know even if it hurts."

Again, I waited.

"Ok, I have to know, so I'll ask you. I guess I want to know if the slipper fits my foot."

"What does that mean?"

"Can I get a real man? I mean a man who doesn't want a baby, and isn't a user. Is it in the cards for me?"

"That's what might hurt?"

"Yeah. I mean, what if I don't have what that kind of man wants? What if I'll always be too young? I know I'm still a bit of a baby. What if I'm just not good enough? I mean, I know what lots of men want from me when they look at me, but I've never felt it's me they want."

"That an awful feeling."

"It is. So, a man who isn't a user, what does he look for in a woman? What do you think? I really want to know."

"I'll tell you what I think. In the best of circumstances, I think what that kind of man wants from a woman is what she can bring into his life."

"Like what?"

"I think a woman can keep the relationship vibrant."

"What does that mean?"

"There's a quality in every relationship of how alive it is. You can't touch it, but you can feel it. Things that are alive, they do need nurturing."

"A woman can do that for herself and for her man?"

"Yes."

"Why shouldn't a man do it too? Why does it have to be only us women?"

"There are men who can do it too."

"I want someone like that." Michelle looked thoughtful. "Is that why relationships don't work? Because nobody's keeping them alive? You're sure that's it?"

"I am. For a woman's part, if she can't generate anything new in the relationship, the man will have nothing to benefit from it. He'll stay unmoved in an important part of his soul. Relationships stagnate when nothing new is created."

"And then people blame each other. Like my parents."

"Exactly."

"God, if only I'd had you to tell me about this when I was growing up. I wouldn't have wasted so much time." She stretched again and then looked at me with a determined expression. "Okay, no more wasting time. I'm ready to hear it straight out. What does a woman have to do to have the man she wants? Don't beat around the bush. Tell me what you think."

"I will tell you. I think 'all' that's required is that she loves him with no hidden agendas, no conditions, none whatsoever. She has to love him for the sake of love alone, not for prestige or a better social standing or for money or security."

"Now I do feel like you're talking about a saint."

"And she can't be with a man to avoid dealing with her fears, especially the fear of being alone. Or to evade facing the need to go on her own journey in life."

"You make it sound just about impossible."

"It certainly is just about the tallest order a woman can face."

"And what about the man?"

"A man who is loved like that experiences a woman's love as a gift from his fate."

"It takes a real man to be interested in that?"

"Certainly."

"To love someone without conditions." Michelle looked at the ceiling. "This all sounds like such a sacrifice. It seems like every woman I know has conditions for her boyfriend or her husband. My sisters are always worried about what my mother and the rest of the family think about their husbands. They're always monitoring their husbands for how things look. They really drive their husbands crazy."

"That's so difficult, isn't it?"

"It is. The women in my family all make a business out of love. But they make sure their men don't know it." She paused and said again, "To love without conditions. The first thing I think of is, to love that way, it might be very painful. You don't have any control. You're really vulnerable."

"Yes, that's a good part of why so many women avoid it."

"But what about the man? Shouldn't he have to love me that way too?"

"Now you can see how easy it is to fall into this trap. You've already fallen back into setting up condition number one: the man must love me in the following way. If you keep tying your own love to how the other person loves you, you will never really be `in' the experience of your own love, and your mate won't know what it's like to receive your full love."

"That sounds very unsatisfying," Michelle hesitated. "Is what you're saying that each partner has to give everything, instead of 50/50?" She grinned. "Ok, there I go again, setting up conditions. I get it." She ran both hands through the sides of her hair. "I'm trying this on," she said. "If you're busy setting up conditions, you're not busy with the love, right?"

"Yes."

"If I'm going to love a man that way, so vulnerable, I'd have to be sure I could trust him. I'd have to be sure I'd made the right choice, really sure. My problem is, I don't think I've ever been that sure about anything."

"Yes, it does throw the emphasis on the rightness of your choice and on your choosing."

"I am sure about one thing. I know I can definitely choose the wrong person."

"Yes, that's why choice in love is so important."

"Because you can love a person, I mean really love, a man who is wrong for you?"

"Exactly."

Michelle was silent for a moment. "So we don't get to choose who we love, that just happens, but we do get to choose whether they're the right or the wrong person to love?"

"Michelle, that's beautifully said."

"It's scary, but it makes me feel better about the whole thing at the same time. I think I do know one more thing about all this. If you're giving up your conditions about the guy, it must be because you're getting something better. I do think I know what you get. It's what I got with Mimi."

"What's that?"

"If you give up your conditions, you get this amazing feeling about yourself that you can really love, isn't it? I mean, really and truly love?"

"Oh yes. Michelle, I think that's exactly it. I think that's the most satisfying feeling a human being can have. There might be nothing greater."

Sitting up straight, she said, "Nobody who knows me would think it, in fact, they'd probably think I'm the last person on earth, but I think I was made to love someone that way."

Chapter Nine—Jeff

The Office of Dr. Yoav Zein. Psychotherapy.

Hours By Appointment.

Friday, April 27, 2012.

On a bright spring day in April, Jeff wanted to tell me about his latest blind date. "My friend Ronnie set me up with this woman Gloria," he said. "I wasn't too thrilled about it. I've been through this before, I always get a big build-up."

"What's that?"

"You know, everyone always makes their friend sound incredible. Ronnie said this woman Gloria is gorgeous and brilliant and what's more, it's amazing how we share the same interests. Ronnie said Gloria is the perfect match for me."

I couldn't help but smile.

"Yeah, my first reaction was oh really, where have I heard that before? But Ronnie said don't be so closed-minded, you have to go out with her at least once, she's like nobody else, she runs her own business, and you won't regret meeting her. I said I wasn't interested, but Ronnie kept at it, like can you take the chance of missing out on someone who could be your soul mate? Oh all right, I said. So I texted this Gloria and she suggested we have lunch at a steakhouse in Midtown. That place is like going back in time a hundred years. There's pictures of wrestlers and boxers on the walls, sawdust on the floor, and red and white table cloths. The waiters are all men about seventy-five years old, and there's a huge menu, longer than your arm, with lots of aged steaks.

"I got there on time, but Gloria showed up twenty minutes late. She was dressed in a sort of clunky grey business suit with big shoulders. It wasn't very flattering. I stood up to shake hands with her and she waved me away and said, 'wait.' She didn't say one word about being late. She called the waiter over and said, 'Gus, two martinis straight up.' He said, 'right away Gloria.' I realized she must be a regular at the steakhouse.

"I started to ask her a question but she held up her hand again, like for silence. I was looking at her in a bit of amazement. She rummaged through her purse and found a mirror and her lipstick and put it on while I was watching. The martinis came and without looking up, she said, 'Gus, my man.' He nodded, and I noticed he didn't put down a menu for her but he gave one to me. She put her fist around the glass and drank it down in one gulp. She just tossed it back. Then she took the second one and drank it in three gulps. She sighed and said, 'Now that's better.' Then she turned and finally looked at me.

"I'd been watching all of this like it was some kind of performance and I was in the audience. It was mesmerizing. Now that she was facing me, she gave me a really long lookover, and she took her time about it. I mean, slow, and up and down. It felt weird, like I was being inspected. I actually thought, if this is what women go through, I can see why they don't like it. She really took her time. Then she leaned her head close and said, 'I want to work for ten more years and make enough money to retire and move to Florida and golf. Every single day. That's me. That's my plan. Now how about you?'

"And I said, really lame, 'well, it's good that you know what you want.'"

"That's not what I asked you," she said.

"I don't have a plan like that."

"What kind of a plan do you have?"

"Actually, I don't have a plan."

"She shook her head and said, 'if you don't have a plan, you won't get anything worthwhile. You'll just get any old thing." She looked right at me with a straight face and said, 'Maybe that's what you want, any old thing?'"

Jeff stopped his story and said, "I felt like getting up from the table right then. What a complete waste of time with this strange obnoxious woman. But I was more astonished than angry. So I said to her, 'do you always go around saying things like that to people you've just met?'"

"She looked straight at me and said, 'I do.'"

"And do people like it?"

"Maybe, maybe not. That's their business, isn't it?"

Jeff stopped telling his story again and widened his eyes. "I was really stunned. I never met anyone like her before. Not in a woman and not in a man. I was trying to get a grip on what was happening. So after that, we were sitting there in a bit of awkward silence, and I was sort of thinking out loud, and I said to her, "Planning is part of your code, I guess."

"My code? What's that?" She looked huffy. "I don't like it when people talk in code."

"Oh, it's just a word I use for how a person lives. What they live by."

"You could say what you mean, couldn't you?"

Jeff looked at me with a slight smile. "It looked like I'd hit a nerve. Then Gus came with a rare steak for her and she started carving it up. I didn't get my meal yet. She didn't look up and she said, 'You ever been married?'"

"No. Have you?"

"No."

"Since she brought it up, I thought it was ok to ask her, 'How about you? Do you want to be married?'"

"Who doesn't want to be married?"

"I think a lot of people don't."

"Why not?"

"It might not be right for them."

"Well, it would be right for me."

"Is it part of your plan?"

"Of course. I plan to get married and have one child. One will be enough."

"When does your plan say that's going to happen?"

"In two years. I'm busy right now."

"What if someone fell in love with you right now?"

"He'd have to wait."

Jeff looked at me and shook his head. "I don't know what got into me, but then I said to her, 'you don't sound like you're the kind of person who's ready for love.'"

"She dropped her fork and knife and stood up and said, 'how dare you say that? Who do you think you are?'"

"Hey, don't take offense, I wasn't being mean."

"Then why did you say that?"

"It just seems like you have a lot going on, and there might not be tons of room in your life for a relationship. Where would you fit it in?"

"She sat down and said, 'If I didn't know you were a total stranger, I'd say you've been talking to my mother.'"

"Why is that?"

"She says the same thing."

"Well, she could be right."

"Then Gus brought her a fresh drink and she put it down and gave me that same sort of look, checking me out. Then she asked me, 'So do you go around saying things like that to people you've just met?'"

"Actually, no, I never do. I just thought you were the kind of person who wouldn't take offense."

"That's what everybody thinks about me. They think I don't have feelings. Well, I do."

"She was tearing up a bit, and then she said, 'So what about you, are you ready for love?'"

"I'm not sure. I'd like to find out."

"So we'll have another date in two years, ok?"

"I was just about to laugh, but I saw she was completely serious so I said, 'Sure.'"

Jeff stopped the story and said, "Part of me wanted to get up and leave and call it a day. Just write it off. And then I thought, there's something going here I could learn from. Like this whole bizarre episode was all happening because I needed to catch on to something. It was like a set-up for my education about life. I guess you know I have that kind of feeling a lot."

"Yes I do."

"So she was rummaging in her purse, like I wasn't there again, and then something came over me, and I looked at her and all of a sudden I could see why she was putting out all this obnoxious stuff, like a skunk spraying everybody. I got it. The whole thing just dawned on me. A huge ray of light came over me."

"What was that?" I asked.

"I saw oh, she's afraid! She's this spunky woman, she's gone a long way in the business world and she did it her way. Ok, bravo. She speaks her mind because she's built that way and that offends lots of people I'm sure, but that's just her style. It's who she is and it won't ever change, but deep down, she's scared nobody will ever love her. I mean love her for who she is, warts and all. I got it. That's what she's about."

"You really tuned in to her, didn't you?"

"I did. I didn't say a word, but after that it was like I suddenly became her best friend. She told me all about her work, and her friends and where she came from. My food finally arrived and while I was eating she looked at me and asked, 'Do you think you're the right man for me?'

"I gulped down my bite, and then I decided to take my time before I said anything. I thought about what I wanted to say. Then I said to her, 'Listen, I might be not the right person for you and you might not be the right person for me, but I admire what you've accomplished.

It's impressive and something to be proud of. I think you're a real person. That's rare. I think the guy who gets you will get someone really special. I hope he finds you or you find him, and you fit him into your plan."

"Now she was tearing up a little bit again and she said, 'Ronnie said you were special too.' She waved Gus back to our table and ordered another drink. Then she turned back to me and asked, 'You sure you don't like golf?'"

"I can take it or leave it."

"What do you like?"

"I'm a fisherman."

"I don't like the water. And I don't eat fish."

"So I said to her, 'There you go.'"

With that last bit of the story, Jeff stretched and seemed to relax. "It turned out we had no shared interests at all, my friend Ronnie was completely off the beam about that one, but we had a nice lunch anyway, really warm and friendly. She told me all about her life and her problems with her mother. Her mother's on her case all the time, especially about not being married. I realized we do have that one thing in common, so I told her how it bothers me that my mother is usually really unfriendly to the women I've brought home for her to meet. Gloria gave me some good things to think about my mother."

"She did?"

"Yeah. She said my mother must have a motivation for being so cold to my girlfriends, and did I know what it was? Did I ever ask my mother what it was about? I told Gloria those were great questions and I'd have to think on them. I actually wondered if my mother would like Gloria. Not as the right woman for me but because she was such a genuine person. It was refreshing how real she was.

"I was even glad we were in that old fashioned restaurant. Gus already knew she wanted that humongous steak without her ordering it, but for me, he'd suggested this really good piece of fish, which surprised me because it was fresh and they didn't overcook it. Everything else was a side order, and they charge you a fortune for some creamed spinach or some fries. She insisted we split the check. When we said goodbye I gave her a big hug. I felt like I wanted good things for her. She really touched something in me. And I think I touched something in her."

"How wonderful."

"Yeah. So that was what started as the worst date ever, but in the end, I learned something huge."

"What did you learn?"

"Well, you know how crazed I am about sex with the right woman? With her, it never came into my mind. Not that she wasn't attractive or anything. I could see she had something appealing underneath it all. I did wonder what makes a woman like her choose clothes that make her look her worst? Anyway, I was so much into the moment while I was with her, I mean she was such an intense person and it was totally absorbing, it was fascinating, and I realized this is what it means to be in touch with a woman, even if she isn't right for you. When I tuned in to her, I felt really close to her."

"Jeff, this is all very promising."

"It is? Why is it promising?"

"You connected with Gloria as a person."

"I did say that, didn't I? Actually, there was something else that happened that I didn't tell you. I wasn't focused on her the whole time.

While Gloria was talking near the end of the lunch, I was sort of half listening and I went into a kind of a daydream. My mind went back to something I did on that last fishing trip in Montana. One morning I took a walk by myself through the brush, and I picked up a big willow branch. I was using it as a walking stick, just going along. Then the ground started getting wetter and mushier, and I came across two streams that were running side by side towards the river. They weren't very deep, but the water was rushing fast over the ground and the rocks. I walked alongside them for a while, and then I took the branch and started to dig a place in between, to see if the two streams would meet. When I was almost done they just shot together, and they started a new stream right down the middle. I was actually surprised it worked. I thought they would probably go down one or the other of the old ones. I could hear the river not far away, and I walked along this new stream until it flowed into the river. For some reason, I felt really satisfied about what happened with the two streams, how I got them to make a new one. The feeling stayed with me for a long time.

"So I was remembering all of that, seeing myself back then, and then my mind came back to where I was, in the restaurant with Gloria talking. Of course she didn't notice I'd been only half listening. Then I realized I was having that same satisfied feeling right then in my lunch with her. I felt really good in that same way. Something came together, and it felt right, and I started wondering, what exactly was it? Even after the lunch, when I got back to work, I thought about that for a long time without coming up with anything. It was on my mind for a couple of days afterward."

"And now?"

"Like I said, I was really stumped for a while. Then I wondered,

what's going on in my life that's like those two streams? What if my
thing with women is like that?"

"What do you mean?"

"I had this one stream where I wanted sex with whoever I could
get it with. It seemed like that was all I had to think about, all I had to
take care of, just pay attention to what was driving me. It should've
been really simple, getting what I wanted. It seemed that way anyway,
so it was always surprising that things never worked out with women.
Not for very long anyway. Then I finally noticed I had this other
stream going. That was the one where I wanted a girlfriend,
somebody I could be with for good, be with for real. You know, have
something permanent. The girl for that couldn't be just anybody, she
had to be the right one for me. So I was living with the two steams
separate. Really, I was living split in two."

"Split in two?"

"Yeah, that was painful. But now I kind of feel like the streams
have met."

"You do?"

"I do. While I was sitting there with Gloria, I thought, well, things
haven't worked with anyone so far. But I do feel like the two streams
can come together, and I didn't know that before."

For a moment it seemed Jeff would stay with the new discovery
and the new feeling, but then he was back to scratching at his beard,
and said, "But I haven't got any actual proof of that, have I?"

"That's true. It doesn't happen until it happens."

As we stood up at the end of the session, Jeff said, "You've said
that before. But I don't want to be like Gloria, closing my eyes and
putting things off into the future with no guarantees. I mean, what if it

doesn't happen? What if it never happens? Isn't it better to face that?"

I was silent.

As he reached the door, Jeff said, "I think that's the number one thing I could learn from Gloria."

"What's that?" I asked.

"Whether you like it or not, when you're talking about making it with another person, you can't plan everything. It either clicks or it doesn't."

Chapter Ten—Michelle
The Office of Dr. Grace Brennan.
Hours By Appointment.

Friday, May 11, 2012.

"How can I stop being bitter about my mother when she keeps doing these things that drive me crazy?" Michelle asked at the start of her session. "Like look at this dress she gave me, can you believe it?" She was wearing a full-length black silk dress with embroidered flowers.

"What do you mean?"

"This dress is what my mother called a 'present.' She made a big deal about it when I came home for dinner last Sunday." Michelle's voice was filled with sarcasm. "It's Shantung silk. She knows I got the message."

"What message is that?"

"My mother and I, we both know what Shantung silk is used for the most."

"What's that?"

"It's for wedding dresses. My mother knows perfectly well I got her message from this nasty little gift. She was telling me how disappointed she is in me because I'm not married. Of course if I called her on it, she'd deny the whole thing. She'd say, you're so touchy Michelle, can't I even give you a gift? She'd say the dress isn't even white, so how could she mean anything about a wedding? Then she'd say it's all in my head and I'm making things up. That's how she operates, you can never catch her out. Sometimes I do wonder if I'm hallucinating the whole thing, you know like she says, making it up. But then I go back to her look. Everybody knows that look."

"What look is that?"

"When I look at my mother, like I did at her last cocktail party, I always think she looks so glamorous. She wants me to look at her that way. She likes it when I admire her. That's the only time she warms up to me. But if I'm not admiring her, then she looks me up and down and there's no mistaking what's going on. Her nose starts to wrinkle up like she just smelled something bad. My sisters say they get the look even worse than I do."

"What does the look mean?"

"It means there I go again, letting her down again. All of us, my sisters and I, we're all a disappointment to her. She's always fretting over it, rubbing her hands over it, agitating. She could be walking through the house humming to herself, but if she sees me, all of a sudden the look comes out and it's like an ice-cold blast. It could freeze your blood. It's been that way ever since I can remember."

"That's so difficult."

"It is." Michelle smoothed her dress. "You know how they say if you're in a hole, stop digging? What I want to know is, how do I stop digging the hole I'm in with my mother? How do I stop being bitter? I don't like myself that way."

"Those are good questions."

"Look, I know my mother can't be the way I'd like her to be. Don't you think that means I should just give up on her?"

"What would you give up on?"

"On wanting to be close to her and getting her approval." She added, "Isn't that another sacrifice I have to make, to grow up?"

"I don't think we can ever just will ourselves to give up on wanting to be close with someone that important in our lives."

"Yeah, you might be right about that. I've never been able to give up on her, even when I wished I could. I want to, but I just can't. One part of me is for it, and one part of me is against it. That drives me crazy. I don't know if there's a way out of it." She ran her fingers up and down the side of the sofa. "So if you're in a hole and you're stuck, what do you do?"

"I know of only one thing to suggest."

"Well, go ahead and lay it on me with your one thing, I'm all ears." Michelle shook her head. "Sorry, I didn't mean to be rude." She paused. "Anyway, you were saying? What's your suggestion?"

"When you're divided against yourself like that, I think you have to keep your problem and your question top of mind until something comes up and tells you what you can do about it. It's an effort to hold steady in the middle of your dilemma, but the effort is what counts."

"That sounds like such..." Michelle paused again. "Ok, I was going to say that sounds like such crap, but I'm sure you must mean something more about it, right?"

"I do. If you really come to the end of your resources about something, it usually means a new thing wants to present itself, but it can only break through when the old ways are cleared out."

"Has that ever happened for you?"

"It has. I've noticed that sometimes the thing I need to know comes to me when I'm half-awake."

"It's amazing that you said that. Before I came today, I was thinking about something I never told you about my mother. Up until I was a teenager, she used to come into my room before I went to sleep and lie down next to me and close her eyes and not say anything. She always looked so wiped out. We'd just lie there without talking, and I'd listen to her breathing. I'd try to breathe in and out when she did, so we'd be together. I'd fall asleep that way with her next to me, and sometimes she fell asleep too. I never said anything about it, and it was like we had a secret between us."

"Secrets are important."

"They are, but I didn't know what it was. I just went along with it because it seemed like I should. In the mornings you couldn't get near her, she was a house afire, all revved up, and she just attacked the day. But at night she collapsed next to me. I could feel there was something really painful going on in her life, but I was a kid and I didn't have any idea of what it was. Not then anyway."

"Of course."

"But now I think I do know. Like I said to her when we were in her kitchen, I think it comes from the ways she's missing love. There's just no place for it in her life. Not with my father or my sisters or with me."

"That's a source of the deepest suffering."

"I know that for sure." Michelle eyes were watery. "But I did think she might be able to be close to me, when she came in and laid down next to me. It never happened but I was always hoping."

"And you're still hoping?"

"Yeah, I never really gave up hope. I always thought the criticism might go away. I wanted that secret part of her to come out and then we'd be really close."

As if it had been gathering force, massing like a flash flood, Michelle suddenly burst into tears and for the first time actually wailed in front of me. She gave a heart-rending cry, and I nearly burst into tears myself. I understood it to be the pent-up pain that our sessions had released, now that she was strong enough to bear it. After a long cry, the sobs began to slow down, and she began wiping her face.

"My Mom," she said between sobs. "My Mom. You know I never call her Mom. I always call her Mother. But when I was little, I did call her Mom. And she called me 'Mi.' It was like we were Mom and Mi." Again the sobs started and she was barely able to get her words out between them. "I thought we were so close when I was little. Maybe we really were. Then she moved away from being close to me, and I started calling her Mother and she started calling me Michelle."

"There was a separation between you?"

"Yes. And it hurt so much."

"And you thought it was because of you?"

"Yes. It got worse and worse as I got older and it just kept on going. She pulled away from me the most when I needed her most. Like with that whole thing with the neighbor." Michelle's sobs began again and she cried out, "Mom, Mom, why can't you like me?" She put her head between her hands and the tears fell onto her dress.

I had a strong desire to reach out to her and comfort her, but an even stronger knowledge held me back. I trusted that this was something she had to go through, something she would get through.

Between sobs, she said, "It seemed like I did something, something really bad, but I never knew what it was."

At last, the pain seemed to subside and she said, "I'm not really bad, am I?"

"Do you still feel that way?"

"No, I don't think so."

With that, she got up and threw the wet tissues into the wastepaper basket by the couch. "Look at my dress," she said. As she sat down, she took a deep breath and sighed several times, and then said, "I guess I must be like my mother."

"How so?"

"I want to be loved without having to do anything to make myself lovable." She gave a half-smile. "Don't think I don't know I'm a handful."

I nodded. She took a long moment to pull herself together, smoothed her dress, fixed her hair, and crushed a new tissue into a ball in her hands.

"I can say this to you and I know you won't laugh."

I waited.

"I know what love is with a dog, but I still don't know what love is with a human being."

"I see."

"So is it really dumb to ask, what is love anyway?"

"That's a big question, isn't it?"

"Yeah. So what do you say it is?"

"It's not the easiest thing to define, is it?"

"No. And thank you for not asking me what I think."

"Ok. I think love is there when you put the other person in the center, without strings attached for them."

"You mean not setting up conditions, like we talked about before?"

"Yes, there's a way of saying it I like the most. Love is putting the other person in the center, without losing your own center. That's the definition I like most."

"Someday you'll have to tell me what that one means." Michelle suddenly looked contrite. "I'm sorry again, I didn't mean to be rude. That just sounds like something my mother would say. She thinks everything she does is for us, but it's not really true. It's all on her terms."

"So you didn't feel in the center of her love?"

"No. Of course, she wouldn't agree, but I do think I know better."

"All right then, now it's important for you to find out what love is, on your own terms."

"Can't argue with that." She took a deep breath and blew it out. "So tell me, what does it feel like to be in the center of someone else's love?"

"Being in the center of someone else's love should feel good."

"Well, it doesn't sound good to me."

"Because?"

"It might be scary."

"Because?" I asked.

"I just told you about it with my mother. All I know about being in the center is when she looks at me, it's like I'm coming up short, there's a big frown, and then a blast. She lets me know she doesn't like what she sees." She looked down at her dress and added, "but once in a while she likes my clothes. Have you ever wondered why I dress the way I do?"

"Yes, I have Michelle."

"When I put on my outfit every morning, I wonder if my mother would be happy with how I look, or would she just have that awful look that says she's so disappointed? When I get dressed and take a last look in the mirror, I wonder, what do you think Mom? Do you think I look nice, are you pleased? I always think if I could just find a way to get my clothes right, then maybe she would look at me with love." Michelle looked down again. "That's why I dress the way I do. I'm always hanging on."

"Hanging on?"

"To the chance my mother and I could still be happy with each other."

Of a sudden, Michelle looked straight at me with her face set and said, "Don't think I'm a fool. I'm not expecting it to happen right away. I'm realistic." Then her face softened. "But maybe someday? Do you think my mother and I could ever have a positive thing going again? Is there anything I can do about it now?"

"As I said, I think we have to wait and see, with an open mind. Wait for something new."

"You really don't know? I mean, you don't know now?"

"No, I really don't. There are things that go on in the love between two people that no one can predict."

"You know that?"

"I know that when it comes to families, and parents and children, disappointments come when we don't keep the appointments that love sets out for us. Unfinished business in love never goes away."

"And that means?"

"That we can never close the door to being surprised."

Chapter Eleven—Jeff

The Office of Dr. Yoav Zein. Psychotherapy.

Hours By Appointment.

Friday, May 11, 2012.

On a warm day in May, after getting comfortable on the sofa and chatting about the weather, Jeff said, "There was one thing about my sex life I never told you."

"What was that?" I asked.

"My first time."

"Yes, you've never mentioned that."

"It was with a girl named Maya. I was a freshman at Columbia and I was desperate to lose my virginity. I might've looked like I was a college student going to classes and hanging out with my friends, but really I was a maniac about having sex for the first time. It was on my mind twenty-four seven. I was always on the lookout for who it might be. I went to parties and danced with whoever was there, and talked to girls in class, but nothing happened. The first term was going by, and I was getting absolutely nowhere. I started to feel really desperate, but nobody knew."

"You didn't tell your friends?"

"No, I didn't say anything. That was probably more of my Dad's code. You know, if something bothers you, keep your mouth shut. Your problems are nobody's business but your own."

"I see."

"So near the end of the term, early in the morning in my physics class, I was half awake and I opened my eyes and there was Maya, sitting across from me, looking at me with a smile. She was very cute, a science major and really smart. She had glasses and she seemed very studious, but once I heard her laugh and it was so sweet, like a bell going up and down. I'd been keeping an eye on her because I'd overheard one of the guys say she had a new boyfriend every month. Sure enough, I saw her walk out with somebody a couple of times, and a few weeks later it seemed she wasn't with him anymore. I had it in the back of my mind that I might wait for her to be over whoever she was with now, and then I could move in on her. And then I did."

As the memory gripped him, Jeff stopped talking, looked out the window, and then picked at his shirt cuff. I waited for him to continue.

"So I did something bold. It reminds me now of what I did later with Lucia. You remember the girl I went up to and danced with at the hall party?"

"Yes, I remember."

"With Maya, that was the first time in my life I was Mr. Action with a girl. I just ran up to her and grabbed her hand and started walking with her. I figured we were heading for her next class. When I held her hand, she just went with it like she was already waiting for me, like it was entirely natural we would be walking along holding hands. I dropped her off, and told her to meet me in the dining hall for dinner. I don't remember what we said at dinner, but afterward we held hands and walked back to her hall without saying a word. I didn't ask where her roommate was. When we got in, she took off her clothes and laid down on the bed naked. I took off mine and then I came right there before I even touched her. I was so embarrassed. I apologized, way too much, but she was very cool with it. She just said it was no big deal, and a while later, we did it. Of course it was over really fast, but in bed with her, lying there with her in my arms, I got so high I actually felt I was touching the sky. I thought, 'this is love. I'm in love.'"

Jeff looked at me and shook his head. "I was completely gone, I mean I was just floating away. After that, we met almost every night in her room. During the day, I was walking around the campus like I was living on the moon. The first weekend we were together, we took a long walk to Central Park and everything seemed so magical. New York seemed like a different city, like I'd never seen it before. I couldn't believe how beautiful everything was. I remember saying how much I loved living here. Every street had something amazing on it, just for us. There was a street mime in front of the Met, and he stopped us, and he got in front of me. He made a huge smile with his hands on his face and kept on making it wider. Then he staggered around on tiptoe with that ridiculous smile on his face. He got what I was about right away. That was easy. Then he stopped in front of Maya and put his hand to his chin like he was studying her. He put his hands in circles around his eyes for her glasses, and he walked around in a circle wiggling his hips like a girl. Then he studied her some more. After that he went over to a guy walking on the street and acted like he was trying to seduce him. And then another guy and another guy. To this day I wonder how he got that about her. But anyway we were laughing so hard. Everything was magic. She seemed like the most beautiful, incredible girl in the whole world. I had this smile on my face all the time. My roommates were teasing me about it, calling me the Love Man."

"So you did tell them?"

"I couldn't help it. They could see I was a completely different person. Of course they thought I was goofy. But I didn't care."

"I see."

"That was about it. Then it was just over."

"What do you mean?"

"We went together for about three weeks, then we just fell apart. We didn't see each other for a few days, and I might have missed a class or two, and then she was off with a new guy after that. There wasn't anything negative. She was friendly when we saw each other around campus. It was like she acted as if nothing happened. I was really upset for a couple of days. I was crazed at night, more than during the day, because I was used to going to see her and now I had nowhere to go, nobody to be with. Of course now I knew what sex was, and I was so horny it was like I was ready to jump out of my skin. But I surprised myself at how fast I got over her. It was like there was this moment with her and then boom, the moment passed. I was back to square one, almost as if I expected it wouldn't last. Back to being alone and miserable. So that was my first time."

Jeff seemed to put the memory back in its place. "I thought I'd better talk about it with you. Like you always say, I think there's a lot in it."

"What do you make of this now?"

"I see now I went for Maya because she was easy."

"That's what you make of it?"

"Yes. I don't like myself for it. It happened because of weakness."

In past sessions, I had often commented on such self-criticism, but this time I was silent, wondering where Jeff would go next with his account of himself.

"I guess if you see something about yourself that happened because of weakness," he said, "the main thing is to learn from it. In the past all I've ever done is beat myself up about being weak. But I guess beating yourself up doesn't help you to learn."

"It never has in my experience. Have you ever seen it work?"

"I can't say it ever helped. I guess it's another habit I picked up from my Dad. But I can't blame him. I made it a habit of my own." Jeff ran both hands through his hair. "It's amazing how things just hang around in your life, sometimes for years, waiting for you to realize what happened."

"So what else do you realize now?"

"I see something kind of stunning now. Everything that's happened to me, with women and sex? I think I've been telling myself a story about it."

"What do you mean?"

"A couple of days ago I was lying in bed, thinking how I should really tell you about my first time with Maya. I was sort of half-awake, and then I sort of saw a parade, all the women I've told you about, they all came flashing through my mind, one after another. Noel and Ellen and Margery and Lucia and even some others I never told you about. Then I thought, why is it so important for me to tell you about everything that went wrong? What's going on with me? And I realized the whole point of my telling you was to get you to buy in to my big story about everything in my life is frustration."

"You wanted to convince me?"

"Yeah, but I must've been trying to convince myself. It's like I've been a salesman for this story about nothing going right about women and sex. Maybe this parade of women going by was trying to tell me something new. I was just so over the moon with Maya, and I've always thought, oh, it was bad because it was short term and it didn't last. Now I wonder, wait a minute, Maya doesn't fit into the story about never getting anything of what I want."

"Something different happened with her, didn't it?"

"Right, something did. And that's what's been waiting for me to figure out, after all these years."

"You certainly did describe something else, not just frustration."

"Yeah, but what was it?"

"Didn't you describe yourself as happy?"

"That is so true. I was really happy, even if it was just for a couple of weeks. For the first time in my life."

"So the possibility of happiness opened up for you with Maya?"

Jeff sighed. "Yeah. It didn't last, but still there was a taste of honey with her. You could go either way with that."

"What do you mean?"

"You could say it was all a delusion, a trick the mind plays on you. You get drunk on love, and then you have plenty of time to sober up."

"Or?"

"Or you could say it was a hint that things that might get better, maybe later on." Jeff was quiet for some time, and I thought he could be arguing both sides to himself. Then he said, "I think we're back to that whole thing about whether I can trust the future."

"Can you say more?"

"I really bought into the idea I was always going to be frustrated, like it was a life sentence. I was really stuck there. I see that now."

"If you can see that now, it must mean you're separating from that unhappiness."

"I guess I must be." Jeff was silent again for a long time. "There's one more thing I wonder about Maya."

"What's that?"

"I keep coming back to the way I felt, like I was living in a different world. Like I told you, it felt so much like we were in the middle of everything."

"The world was there for you?"

"That's it. It was all there just for us."

"You'd like to feel that way a lot more?"

"You're right. I think I've been going around like it's other people's world, it's everybody else's world, but it's not mine. I think that was the biggest thing missing for my Dad too. He didn't think it was his world, so he didn't make use of what the world has to offer. It was how he lived and how he died."

After scratching his beard and picking at his sleeve button, Jeff asked, "Is it just me who needs to feel this way?"

"No, I don't think so. I think we all need to feel it's our world."

"You can feel that way and still leave space for other people to feel the same way?"

"Exactly. We all need to have the strongest feeling our life is just for us, and that the life around us is just for us too. Without that feeling, we aren't properly situated in our own lives. You got a taste of that with Maya. Of course, you would have to be frustrated if that feeling escaped you afterward."

"I was frustrated because I couldn't quit going after being happy?"

"Yes, it can sound strange, but I think your frustration saved you."

"It did?"

"Being agitated about not getting what you want was the sign you hadn't given up on the better things of life. You still had the vision of a better world, calling to you, and so your frustration was the indication you still had a lot of energy to go after what you needed."

"Wow, that's a new one."

We were silent for quite some time. At last Jeff said, "But I haven't got any proof it's right to feel it's my world. It seems like it could be a serious mistake. I can't take your word for it, even though I really want to. I need proof."

"For that kind of thing, there's only one kind of proof."

"What's that?"

"The proof of your own experience."

"I'm glad you said that. I wouldn't have believed anything else."

Chapter Twelve—Michelle
The Office of Dr. Grace Brennan.
Hours By Appointment.

Friday, May 25, 2012.

Michelle arrived for her session in an eggshell white lace dress with an empire waist and a flared hem. She was visibly excited, wanting to talk about something that happened that was "fun, but scary." As she started to talk, I noted to myself that, unlike the sour disappointment that characterized so many of her previous sessions, today's mood of enthusiasm had in fact become more prevalent.

She began by reminding me about her friend Ronnie, who worked for the same multimedia company, but at a travel magazine on a different floor. "So Ronnie finally got her degree and she invited me to her graduation last week. It was at the Javits Center. Before the ceremony, I was helping her with her cap and gown, and she introduced me to this guy Jeff. He works at a newsmagazine on a different floor in our building. Then Ronnie left to get ready for the ceremonies and I was all alone with this guy."

Michelle said she was off to the side, just chatting with Jeff while

Ronnie's proud relatives were in the row below them. "We were talking about how great it was that Ronnie got her college degree while holding a full-time job. We were gabbing away," Michelle said, "and then the musicians began to play, and the procession started and the graduates started walking in, and everyone stood up. I had to move a bit to my left to get a better view, next to Jeff. We started whispering. I said, 'I get goosebumps when they come to the slow part of Pomp and Circumstance.'"

"The whole thing gives me goosebumps," he said.

"Why do you suppose that is?" I asked him.

"I think it's because there's always a part of us that wants to graduate too," he said. "You know, even if we've got a college degree, maybe we still have the feeling there's something else we need to graduate about."

"I like that," I said. "I've never heard it put exactly that way before."

Michelle stopped her story and said, "even though I was staring straight ahead at the ceremony, it was so nice being next to this guy. Kind of rubbing shoulders. He's the first thoughtful guy I've met in a long time. So I wanted to say something more to him. So I said, "Maybe we get goosebumps from the pride.'"

He turned to her and seemed about to say something in response, but just then Ronnie came into view, and her friends and family began to wave wildly. The speeches, awards, and conferral of diplomas began.

Sitting next to Jeff for so long, Michelle said, was something she wished had gone on even longer. He was trim and athletic-looking, she said. He had a high forehead and deep-set brown eyes. He wore an open blue-checked shirt with a grey suit that had a tailored look. She said he seemed perceptive, in the most intriguing way.

After the ceremony, drinking lemonade and chatting with the family of the happy graduate, he turned to Michelle and asked her a question. He said it had been on his mind during the long ceremony.

"What did you mean about the pride?" he asked.

Michelle flushed and shrugged and bent over her lemonade.

"No, I'd like to know," Jeff persisted.

Michelle straightened up. "I think pride gets a bad knock," she said. "Most of the people I know need more of it, not less of it." Then she added, "But for the right things of course."

"Yes, you can't do much without a bit of pride," he said.

That was the end of their conversation, but Michelle said the episode left her with a good feeling. Finishing her account of what happened at the graduation, she smoothed her elegant white dress, took her feet out of her shoes, and pulled at her stockings.

"That was fun talking to that guy," she said. "I've been thinking I want things to go better in my life, and I want more fun like that. What if I was wrong to think everything always has to turn out lousy with men?" She curled her feet under her dress. "So let's talk more about how to meet the right man, ok?"

"Ok."

"So what's the best way to do it? I've tried getting fixed up by my girlfriends and my sisters and it's always been a dud. The last blind date I had, the guy met me at a restaurant, and he came in and talked about himself for an hour, bragging about how much money he made and where he went to school and dropping names of famous people. I got sick of it and I said to him, 'I don't mean to be rude but if you're trying to impress me it's not working.' That seemed to stop him in his tracks for maybe three minutes and then he started up again, so I made up an excuse about having to visit my grandmother in the hospital and left." She made a face. "I've been on a lot of awful dates. It's torture."

"That was no picnic."

"You got that right."

This time it was my turn to introduce a surprising new topic.

"Do you know how to play chess?"

"What does that have to do with it?"

"Do you?"

"Sort of."

"Do you remember what it means for a pawn to capture another pawn en passant?"

"It moves over sideways?"

"Yes, and into the space the other pawn has just moved over. The rules of the game are if you don't make that move just then, you lose the chance to do it for the rest of the game."

"Ok, so?"

"So I think the best way to meet a man is en passant. If you're fully engaged in the game of life, going forward on your path, occupied with things you enjoy and you find fulfilling, and you accept yourself in some basic way without the condition of being with a man, then when a suitable man comes by, you can shift lanes while still going forward."

"And do you capture a man?"

"Well, that's a loaded topic. Again, it's a scandal to say it, but I think it's part of the way men and women are meant to relate to each other. When you give yourself unconditionally, as we've talked about, without the hidden desire to hook a man, it does change the way the world relates to you. Of course, you can't do it for the effect it has, because that would be back to the old fashioned kind of manipulation."

"Controlling."

"Exactly. But when you are truly loved, you are also captured. Not by the other person, but by love itself."

"I like that," Michelle said. "En passant, huh?" She added, "But you said it only works if you're really in the game of life?"

"Yes."

"Well, do you think I'm in the game of life?"

"Do you?"

"I don't think I was. I was on the sidelines. But maybe now I'm in the game of life at work."

"You are?"

"I think so. There was this project editor at work, and I was helping him out a lot. Totally on my own, nobody told me to do it. A month ago I walked into his office and asked him if there were any full-time jobs available. He gave me a really fast brush off, and I was really upset and ready to say something nasty to him. But I didn't. I went back to my desk to pout. That's what I've always done. But I was sitting there and I thought, Michelle where has that gotten you? Is that the way you want to be? C'mon, be real, does that work? So I just swallowed how much I wanted to bite him, and I kept on volunteering my time for him, and he came back and said I could help out on this rush project that was taking up everyone's time. I stayed really late and came in earlier than everyone else for the next couple of days.

When we met the deadline and everybody was congratulating themselves, he said there's a chance I could get hired full time, but I'd have to work with this team of women. They're mostly younger than me, but they're called 'Senior Article Planners.' It's funny, they're called SAPs. They're a tight little clique, like the cool girls in high school. They're bitchy to everyone except the bosses. So he asked me, 'do you think you can handle it?' And I was really proud of myself because I thought of what to say back to him."

"What did you say?"

"I said 'isn't the important thing whether you think I can handle it?'"

"And he said, 'ok, you can come on board but you'll have a three-month probation period. If you can't cut it, we'll know long before then."

"So he's giving you a chance?" I asked.

Michelle sighed. "He is. I have to work around those girls in order to get my job done," she said. "It's really draining. After work I go home, make supper and go right to bed. But I have to say I'm not bored anymore. I am learning something." She added, "So there it is, I'm a full-time employee. Doesn't that mean I'm in the game of life?"

"Michelle, congratulations, but how come you haven't told me about this before?"

"I'm sorry, I didn't mean to keep you out of the loop. I just didn't really believe it was happening, even when it was."

"I see."

"Now that I'm telling you about it, maybe something like that did happen with this guy Jeff, the one I met at Ronnie's graduation. Couldn't he be a man I met en passant? Maybe I just didn't really believe it with him either?"

"Will you see him again?"

"Maybe."

We had reached the end of the session. At the door, Michelle added, "I feel like I'm on probation with men too. My new rule is three months of consistent dating with any man before any sex."

At our next session, Michelle arrived in a tailored two-piece suit in bright white-and-pink plaid. Her heels were two-toned in matching pink and white. The previous week she'd said from now on she was only going to wear suits to work because she wanted the world to know she was a businesswoman, however fashionable. This time even before sitting down, she talked so excitedly that I had to slow her down.

"I was walking into work," she said, "and I saw that guy I'd met, Jeff, in the crowd and he scrambled through to get near me, and he reached out and grabbed my elbow and he said, "Hi, how've you been?"

"Good," I said. "Talked to Ronnie?"

"No, I've been kind of busy, but I really should call her. Listen, are you free for lunch?"

"No, I've got a meeting," I said. "But I'm free for lunch tomorrow."

"Oh, I've got a meeting tomorrow. How about dinner tonight then?"

"I can't, I've got to work late," I said. "But I'm free for dinner tomorrow."

"Oh, no, I'm tutoring some kids tomorrow night," he said.

So I turned to him and I said, "You aren't busy Friday night, are you?"

He shook his head.

"Then come to my place for dinner."

"All right," he said.

After telling me with evident pleasure about meeting this new guy again, Michelle said, "I'd just met this guy and already I invited him over to my place for dinner. I must be totally out of control. I almost felt sick about it afterward."

"You felt sick?"

"I did. I don't know what I had in mind, inviting him to my apartment."

"What did you have in mind?" I asked.

"Well, all right, I guess I already had in mind seducing him," Michelle said.

"Into what?"

"Into bed, what else?"

"Yes, but I think you might've had something else in mind too."

"What do you mean?"

"I think you wanted to test something," I said.

"What?"

"A way of relating."

"What do you mean?"

"Well, as you described it, he was forthright in asking you out and you responded in kind. You were quite frank, and you asked for what you wanted. But now you're uncertain if that was the 'right' approach. Weren't you trying out this more direct side of yourself? Haven't you said you want that freedom in a relationship, if it's going to suit you?"

"You're right," Michelle said. "I don't want to be like my mother and my sisters. I want to be free to be myself. And like you said, I want to be direct. And it's got to be okay with him too."

"Sure."

"So is there anything wrong with a woman being direct?"

"A lot of people think so. There's a very long history of criticism and even rejection, in many cultures, of women who are direct. I think it's something that every woman should be aware of, even if she wants to live her life in a completely different way."

"It's so amazing you said that, because of what happened at the dinner."

"What happened?"

Michelle said she decided to make dinner for this young man herself. She fretted for hours about what to wear and what to cook. In the end, she chose a simple black A-line skirt with no pleats and a flowery blouse. Despite the fact that she ordinarily ordered her dinner from a series of take-out menus that she rotated in a folder in a kitchen drawer, Michelle said she did have something of a knack for cooking. She made a large salad that she served in wooden bowls and a vegetable lasagna that she served on clear glass plates. He brought a small bouquet that she put on the dinner table, and he brought a bottle of Barolo that he said he had special ordered from his local liquor store.

For the first part of the meal, the talk was mostly about their jobs, and they told each other about their current projects. Michelle said she was "incredibly pleased" to discover she had a lot to say to him about her "creative ideas" at work, and that Jeff had many questions and seemed quite impressed. For his part, he said a recent promotion had taken him by surprise, and he was really happy to share his good news with his mother, who was in an assisted living facility and was fighting several illnesses.

"I was really touched that he talked so tenderly about his mother," Michelle said. "I told him I never talk about my mother that way. He asked how come? Then I told him I don't get along very well with my parents and he seemed genuinely sorry about it. I was kind of shocked to see myself through his eyes."

"You usually don't like to have people feel sorry for you."

"You're so right. But coming from him, it seemed okay."

"It was okay?"

"Yeah, I was thinking, if he gets along with his parents, naturally he would think someone like me has missed out on things. He asked why we don't get along? I said my parents can be very cold people when it comes to their children, and even to each other. But they work like a well-oiled team on everything about their ambitions. I said I learned not to get in their way."

"What was his response?"

"He looked genuinely sorry. I thought, this guy is a real human being. He can be tender. Then he really surprised me. It was one of a lot of surprises."

"There were others?"

"There were. He asked me, "Do you mind if I say something about your parents?""

"No, go ahead, go for it," I said.

"I think your parents missed a golden opportunity," he said. "Someday I bet they'll regret it. Remember how we were talking about pride, at the graduation? I think it's the greatest thing in the world, a real source of pride, to be a parent. I mean, to be a good one. I've been thinking about it a lot because my Dad and I never really connected and I only found out why very recently.'"

"What do you mean, you found out?"

"My Dad died when I was in college. He wasn't very talkative and he kept all his thoughts to himself. I was cleaning up my Mom's house a while ago and I found some of his old letters. I showed them to my Mom and I asked her if she knew he loved her even though he never said it to her. She said he didn't have to say it, she knew it. That was good enough for her. That's the way she's built. But I didn't know that growing up."

"You didn't know what?"

"That somebody could be thinking about you, even love you, but never say anything about it. That's not my style."

"So that's not what you want for yourself, like in a relationship?"

"You got it. I want to know what the other person is feeling, and I want them to know what I'm feeling. I've had enough of walking around in the dark in life. We were given the power of speech so we might as well use it."

"Is that what you're looking for in a woman?"

"It is. I haven't been very successful in finding it. Relationships have been my sore spot. What about you?"

"It's the same for me."

"How come?"

"I've always said two things don't work out in my life. Men and my career. Now that I've got a good job..."

"Maybe things can change?"

"That's right."

"Why didn't things work out, with men?"

"I could say I just didn't meet the right one. But that would be only part of the story."

"What's the other part?"

"I wasn't ready. I didn't know how to be close to someone. I wasn't close to myself."

"That's amazing. That's exactly what I've found out. There's all these things I didn't know about myself. It's like there was a book about me, and I'd never read it."

"Would you ever share some of what's in it?"

"I just did."

There was an awkward moment of silence.

"Ok, that's my cue to say it's time for dessert," Michelle said. "Come into the kitchen." She put a bamboo cutting board and a bowl to the side of the sink. "Can you peel these peaches for me?" she asked. "This is a good paring knife."

"I've never heard of peeling peaches."

"Try it. You'll like it."

The skin of the peaches almost slid off under the knife. When he was done, she sliced the peaches into bowls and poured over a small amount of cream. They sat down again at the dining table.

"This is the first time in my life I'm eating peaches and cream," he said.

"How is it?"

"I feel drunk. But I'll have a second helping."

When he was finished, he walked into the kitchen with the bowls and placed them in the sink and she followed him. Then he turned and reached for her hands and she held them out. He pulled her in, held her tight and kissed her. She kissed him back, and then relaxed in his arms and smiled. "Here?" she said. "Now?"

Michelle stopped telling her story. "That's the only time in my life I've ever been direct about sex. It felt completely natural. And you won't believe what happened next. A really big surprise."

"What happened next?"

"So we stopped kissing and he started shaking his head and he said, "'I can't believe I'm doing this twice in my life, but I think we'd better wait.'"

"Why do you say that?"

"Because we need to get to know each other better. There'll be time enough for everything," he said.

"You can really wait?" I was incredulous.

"Barely," he said. He was smiling. "Don't push me."

Michelle finished giving me the "dish" on the date with a sigh. "It's definitely a first for me," she said. "This is the only guy who has ever turned down sex with me. It's always the other way around."

"How does it feel?"

"I thought I'd feel rejected but I don't. Actually, it feels great," Michelle said. "We're going fishing on the weekend and we have separate rooms." Michelle added, "I've never been fishing before. I hope I like it."

There was a bit more to the story, she said. She walked him to his bus stop and they kissed again for a long time on the street. Now there was a new concern, she said. Concentrating at work was becoming a challenge. It was a test of her ability to put aside her riotous daydreaming about what might happen next with Jeff.

Chapter Thirteen—Jeff

The Office of Dr. Yoav Zein. Psychotherapy.

Hours By Appointment.

Friday, June 15, 2012.

"There's a new chapter in my life with women," Jeff said. He was smiling as he sat down.

"What happened?" I asked.

"I met this girl."

"Can you give her a name?"

"Michelle. I met her at a graduation ceremony. She's very hot." Jeff shook his head at his own words. "Ok, I find her very hot."

He went on to describe her as having an open and pretty face with light-colored eyes ("I think they're blue or maybe blue-green"), very stylish clothing, and an energetic and unusually straightforward way of talking. "She doesn't beat around the bush," he said. "She says what's on her mind. I like that a lot. It gets to me. That's why this is so bizarre."

"What's bizarre?"

"I asked her out and we couldn't get free at the same time on the weekdays, so she made dinner for me at her apartment at the end of the week. When I got there, I felt a little bit like it was a setup."

"What do you mean?"

"When I walked in, I saw she had candles lit up all around the apartment and the room lights were turned down. The mood was really romantic. I kind of laughed to myself. I was thinking, yeah, this is what women do when they want to set you up. I have to say it worked, the mood got to me. Right away, I felt a little of that magic feeling I told you about before. Her little apartment was sort of an oasis. I haven't been in a place like that for a long time."

Jeff stopped his story, and as often happened, seemed lost in his memory. After sighing, he continued.

"So I brought a good bottle of wine. It turns out she's something of a cook and we had a great meal. We sat at the table after we ate and talked until late. We just clicked. It was like we tuned in to the same wavelength. We couldn't tell each other enough about ourselves. I told her about my Dad and my promotion, even a little bit about how I've been messed up about women. She didn't say anything about any of her relationships from the past but she did tell me about her parents. They're political, I think I've read about them. She makes them out to be pretty bad. I wondered if she could be seeing them upside down like I did with my Dad. But I didn't say anything about it."

"Too soon?"

"Right. Anyway, she's got this new job. She really likes what she's doing and it sounds very cool. She said it's the first time in her life where she's making an impact. We were talking and I lost track of time and then I realized it was really, really late and we were in her kitchen and I just wanted to kiss her. So I took her hands and wrapped her in my arms. It was a kiss I've been waiting for my whole life. It was so right. I didn't feel anything inside against it. It was just a kiss between me and a woman who was right for me to kiss. It was very long, I mean really long, and I could sense she was giving me the green light, she was ready to go to bed with me. But then something came over me and I told her we'd better wait."

"You did?"

"Yeah, I said to her, I can't believe I'm doing this twice in my life. Of course, she had no idea what I was talking about." Jeff shook his head back and forth. "I'm not at all sorry I did it, but it's bizarre how this keeps happening to me."

"How come you told her to wait?"

"You know, there's a part of me that wants to say I just did it, and that's all there is to it. But by now, I know there's no such thing. You always say every action has a motivation. So ok, I think I wanted to wait because it felt like it would have been putting the cart before the horse."

"Go on."

"I mean, I know I'm going to sleep with her. I'm really sure of it, and I'm pretty sure it's going to be great. But I'm greedy. I want more. It's all got to be great, every last part of it. Everything's got to go right for the first time in my life. We've got to get off on the right foot, and stay right. I want the whole thing. I want everything possible from it. I won't settle for less."

"You're determined."

"I am. Sleeping together at the wrong time could actually interfere with the whole thing. It could interfere with what I want, the whole thing about sex and being together." He stopped shaking his head. "Yeah. It was just too soon, on the first night."

"So not a cause for frustration?"

"I don't know about that. Like I said, I'm glad I did it but I'm on fire for her anyway. But I wonder about something."

"What's that?"

"Why was she ready to sleep with me?"

"You want to know if she was going to put the cart before the horse?"

"Yeah, I hope it doesn't mean she does that all the time."

"Then she wouldn't be the right one for you?"

"Exactly. You know girls who sleep with you on the first date are always what guys say they want, but then there's this thing about those kind of girls aren't keepers, they're just easy, and I suppose they want to please, but it isn't really appealing, not even to guys like Mike."

"It worries you?"

"It does. I wonder, what was her motivation? Do you think I could ask her?"

"What would be at stake?"

"I'm not sure. We hardly know each other. She might take it the wrong way. Like I was criticizing her."

"That's a real possibility."

"But if I can't ask, how can I know?" Jeff ran his hands through his hair. "This is new for me. I never had a girlfriend I could ask things like that. Sometimes I wonder if there's any such thing as a woman you could talk to that way."

"This would be a new way to relate to a woman?"

"Yeah. Asking what I want to know. Do you think that's what I've been missing? I mean, for the millionth time, why do I always get into things like this?"

"It's an interesting question, isn't it?"

"I think there's a risk so I better wait for the right moment to ask her." Jeff seemed to have settled the question for himself and then went on to talk about his mother, who was adjusting slowly to her new assisted living residence. "She doesn't ask me to visit her," he said, "but if I miss a weekend, the next time she looks so down. It's heartbreaking." The session was drawing to a close and as he left, he said he would in fact be disappointing his mother that weekend, because he asked Michelle to go fishing with him on an overnight trip to the Salmon River in upstate New York, near Lake Ontario.

In the next session he sat down, scrolled to find a photo on his phone, and then handed the phone to me. He said the photo was from the fishing trip, with the two of them dressed in wading boots and floppy fishing hats, holding a huge salmon together.

"What do you think of her?" he asked.

"It's a wonderful photo. I see how she's looking at you." I handed the phone back to him.

"Yeah, she is wonderful, isn't she?" He looked contented as he put the phone back in his pocket. He opened a black briefcase and asked if it would be okay if he gave me a present, which always raises questions of appropriateness in the therapeutic setting.

"What prompts the question?" I asked.

"I'd like to say thanks for what happened."

He took out the present for me. It was a dove, beautifully hand-carved in walnut. I accepted it with gratitude. But before I could ask if there was a special significance to the dove, Jeff was eager to continue his account of the trip with Michelle.

"So we drove up on Saturday and we talked in the car non-stop. When we talk, the time just flies by. The photo is from just before dinner. The fish aren't really spawning yet. I fixed the rods with streamers and wet flies. I didn't take her out in a boat, not on her first time. I showed her how to be a bank angler on a gravel stream. I brought boots for her so she could go in and feel the river." Jeff said the water had two-foot visibility and was slightly turbid. "I wanted to wade deeper in the water, like I do when I'm by myself, but I wanted her to be comfortable and I guess I wanted to be close to her even more."

Jeff said they stopped talking for quite a while, listening together to the sound of the river moving over the rocks.

"I was standing there with her, and the water was rushing by. It was a magical moment. I was thinking, I've got this beautiful girl with me and she's smiling, and she's really happy in overalls and boots, even though she dresses more fancy than any girl I've ever known. It's one of the happiest moments of my life. I thought I'm not going to ruin it by asking why she was ready to sleep with me. It's not the time or the moment. So I said, 'Michelle, I like you.' And she smiled back at me. 'And I said, no, Michelle, I really, really like you.' And she said, 'I like you too, Jeff. I really, really like you too.'"

Jeff was beaming as he told me of this special moment.

"There was no problem saying that to each other. It was like there was a match with the river and with us, there was a flow between us. It was like we already knew that we really, really like each other. But saying it out loud added another dimension. It was what I've been looking for my whole life."

"You were creating a moment."

"Exactly. That's what I've learned here, with you. How to create moments. How important it is to create moments."

"That's wonderful, isn't it?"

"It really is. And you won't believe what happened next."

"What happened next?"

"So we were standing there in the water, not talking for a very long time, but really just there with each other, and she suddenly got very serious and she said, 'Listen, I've got to ask you something and of course you don't have to answer it, but I've got to ask.' Her face got red and she said, 'Did you have the feeling I was ready to sleep with you, after dinner at my place?'"

Jeff looked at me for my reaction. I waited, and he continued. "I was just amazed. Blown away. In shock. I had the weirdest feeling. It was like my life was rushing ahead of me just like the water in the river and it was going so fast that I could barely keep up."

"What does that mean?"

"It's like I caught a glimpse of something. Like there is a plan in my life, arranging a lot of things, and I saw it's always been ahead of me. I could see it's always heading for what I need, not always for what I want. This time the plan of my life was only one step ahead of me and I could see it before it got away from me again. I was thinking, 'Does this woman know what she is doing? Is this really happening? Is this for real?'"

"What did you say?"

"I asked her why she wanted to know if that's what I was feeling. I really couldn't think of anything else to say. And she said 'because I want you to know me better. And I want to know you better. If you don't know the reason why I was ready to sleep with you, I'll feel like you don't know what happened, what's going on in me. And I want you to know.'"

"I said 'You don't have to tell me.'" Jeff stopped telling the story, laughed, scratched his chin, and said to me, "Of course I wasn't really being honest. You know I was dying to hear what she had to say." He resumed the story.

"So she said, "Well, if you feel that way, like you don't have to know, that's your privilege. But I do feel like it's our business together. Like I said, I want you to know me."

"I said, 'then go ahead. I'm listening. The fish are listening too.'" Jeff interrupted the telling of the story again and said, "It was kind of lame, but I had to say something because I felt so tense."

Jeff said that Michelle "has a wild laugh," and she just threw her head back. She said, "Jeff, what you did was a first for me. Guys have always wanted to sleep with me whether I was ready for it or not."

"With somebody who looks like you, I can see why."

"Thanks for the compliment." She smiled. "Ok, so if I'd done that two years ago, if I'd gone to bed with you right away, I would've done it because I would've been afraid of losing you. And I wouldn't have even known that was why I was doing it."

Jeff nodded.

She went on. "Whenever I've done that, things turned out badly. I've learned a lot about myself from the mistakes I've made. Especially those kind of mistakes."

"What kind of mistakes?"

"Doing things because I was afraid to say what I feel. Afraid even to know what I really feel. Keeping what I feel a secret from myself."

"I think I know a lot about those kinds of mistakes," Jeff said. "But I still don't get what you mean."

"You said you only recently found out what was going on with your Dad? And there was a lot going on? Well, I only recently found out something that was going on in me. It's like there was another person inside me, and I was blocked from knowing what that person wanted. Everything I did just led me off the trail of what I really needed. I always thought I was good at putting other people off the trail, like keeping my mother and my sisters from coming at me, but it was really me doing it to myself. But this time, with you, it's different. I'm ready for you now. I've been ready for you for a while."

"Ready, huh?"

"Ready."

Jeff said he was in turmoil. Was he ready himself? Was she overconfident, fooling herself? Did she know about the risks? Couldn't getting close be another mistake, a really big mistake this time? Just then, two white birds flew overhead down the course of the river and then into the trees.

"Did you see that?" he asked Michelle.

"Yes, what were they?"

"They were doves. I've never seen them fly together like that before."

"Is it a sign?"

"Maybe, but of what?"

"Yes, of what?" She added, "Don't they mate for life?"

"I'm pretty sure they do."

"So they can manage it?"

"I don't think they have to manage it," Jeff said. "It's natural for them."

"What about for us?" she asked.

"Maybe there's a part of us that's like doves," he said.

With that, the talking stopped. The afternoon sun went behind the trees, and they hiked back to their cabins. As they walked, they could hear the cooing of the doves. Michelle said she needed a nap, and they agreed to meet at the barbecue pit for dinner. Jeff went back to his cabin and sat in the Adirondack chair on the porch. He thought about the upside-down nature of his life, and how this could be one more episode in a long history of things unfolding in a way he never expected. Or maybe not? Was there a plan or wasn't there?

Later, after he split and cleaned a King salmon and Michelle wrapped the fish in herbs and roasted it in tin foil on a bed of coals, they sat next to each other on a picnic bench and ate a meal in silence. After they cleaned up the dinner and sat down again, he said, "You know, I appreciate what you told me this afternoon. It took guts." He didn't look at her and stared straight ahead. "Okay, so I'll tell you something about myself too," he said. "I've made a lot of mistakes too, with women. I've been hot for the wrong ones. Once I realized that, I've practically dedicated my life to getting over it."

"Was that why you didn't want to sleep with me?"

"No with you, it was just the opposite."

"What do you mean?"

"It was because I wanted you, and I felt like you could be the right one."

He turned to her and they kissed for a long time until the night air became chilly. At last they got up and went to their cabins.

As Jeff finished this last part of his story, he sighed again. He said for those two days of the weekend, he was the closest he had ever been to another human being. During their time together he talked about himself openly and he heard about Michelle's life in some of its most intimate details. "I think the closest she's ever been to anyone was her dog, when she was growing up," he said. "But the dog died and she said she's felt alone since then. She's an intense person. I could feel her hunger for me."

"You could?"

"Yeah. She's as hungry to be close to me as I am to her." He said there was "tremendous sexual tension" hovering between them, but the tenderness between them was a "peak" experience of his life.

As our session drew to a close, he said that waiting to sleep with Michelle had been the right way to start out with her, but he didn't want to wait much longer.

"So you're ready?" I asked.

"I am," he said at the door. "Enough is enough."

Chapter Fourteen—Michelle
The Office of Dr. Grace Brennan.
Hours By Appointment.

Friday, June 29, 2012.

"Fishing was great, kissing was better," Michelle said in our next session. She was in a rush to give her account of what happened with Jeff on their weekend trip together. I noticed that her sleeveless black and red floral sundress gave her a breezy look. She looked happier than I had ever seen her.

"We had a great time together. It was a little intense, talking about our past and filling each other in on the things we've been through, but I loved every minute of it. For the first time I felt like the guy I was with was actually interested in me. With guys who just wanted sex from me, I always had this feeling of being picked at. But Jeff's really attracted to me, not just the idea of getting into my pants. It's kind of overwhelming. It feels like a power I have but it makes me uncomfortable. Why do you think that is?"

"What's your idea?"

"It's like now I know for the first time when you attract a man, you have power." Michelle looked at me for my response and said, "Ok, ok, I know you'd want me to say it differently. It's me. I'm the one. When I attract a man, I have power."

"What about that makes you uncomfortable?"

"I guess I'm worried I need to use the power, you know, use the power over the guy to make him stay. The women I know say you have to hold on to a man or he'll leave."

"But you're not comfortable with that?"

"Oh God, no. I know how much that causes problems. I don't want to hold onto him and I don't want to control him. My mother does that. She never lets Daddy see her without her make-up. She controls everything he sees and she's out to control everything he does. Ugh. I just don't want to live that way." She took a moment to formulate her thoughts. "How do you stop doing that, controlling a man?"

"Yes, how do you stop?"

"You'd have to be sure that your partner really does find you attractive no matter what you look like? I mean, if you give up trying to make him feel he wants to stay with you, what do you do instead?"

"You're looking for confidence in why he would stay with you?"

"Yes, that's it. What would you say in the case of Jeff?"

"Why don't you try it?"

"I know he finds me physically attractive," Michelle said, smiling. "Sure."

"But I know that can't be enough to really hold us together."

"Then what could?"

"I know I'm a person now, and I have my own point of view about things. I worked hard to get that, and I'm not giving it up. But what does that have to do with holding us together? I guess I don't know much about it. What do you think it is?"

"I think the power of the bond of love will always have something mysterious in it. We never know everything about it, but we can trust a relationship if the love is enhancing the life of our partner."

"And if the partner knows it?"

"Yes, very much so."

"So back up for a minute. If a person is like my mother, and doesn't trust the power of love to keep you and a man together, then you go for the other kind of power instead? The controlling one?"

"That's the way it works, isn't it?"

"I guess that must be about right," Michelle said. "On the trip, Jeff told me about some major wrong turns he's taken in life, and you and I both know I sure have my own share of wrong turns. We've both had a lot of problems with love. And I can see we've both had confidence problems about it. But it does seem like neither one of us want to control the other. Aren't we lucky to have met each other despite all the wrong turns?"

"Without question."

"I feel something I've never felt before. It feels weird," Michelle said. She was quiet a moment while staring at me.

"What's that?" I broke the silence.

"I think I feel grateful."

Our smiles at each other were now a regular part of most of Michelle's sessions.

"You know, this is a fantastic thing for me," she said. "I understand totally why I couldn't make things work with any guy until now. I just wasn't at the place where I could handle something like this. I wouldn't have known how to enhance my own life or anybody else's. I had to get down and dirty into the crap in my life before things could get better. It felt like it was just me who had to do that, nobody else, but after Jeff told me about himself, I wondered. Maybe it's not just me?"

"No, you're not the first to have that experience."

"I'm not?"

"In the Song of Songs, the bride compares love to the shyness of a gazelle, and says not to call up love before its time."

"Because it will flop if you go for love before you can handle it?"

"Exactly. The warning isn't heeded much in our time."

"I could've really used the warning."

"Yes, with love there should always come some knowledge of what's necessary to make it work. People in our time don't ask the question of whether they are ready for love. Or what they might need to do to get prepared for it."

"I like that a lot. Not before its time. I guess my time has come."

With this extraordinary statement, I felt the moment called for a summing up, not just of this discussion but of our work together. "Yes. You did what was necessary. As you said, becoming a person. I would add, becoming a whole person. That is what heals." I added, "That's what makes the time right."

There was silence for a moment, and then she was clearly thinking of something else. "Do you think there's anything wrong with having a little fun with him?"

"What do you mean?"

Michelle said that she and Jeff had lunch together in the employee cafeteria in the middle of the week. In contrast to what she said was the serious tone of their conversation during the fishing trip upstate, their talk at lunch was full of humor and banter. As they reached the cashier, he said, "my treat" and paid for both of their meals. They sat down to eat, and he picked over the salad makings on his plate. Michelle said, "Not as good as the one at my place?"

Jeff said, "Definitely not. But I haven't tasted everything of yours."

"You want to sample everything on my menu?"

"That would be very satisfying."

"Hmmm. Do you think you can afford it?"

"Would you care to look over my bank account with me?"

"No, you look like a man I can trust with my precious goods."

"Ah, there's that word again," he said. "Trust. That's the basis of everything, isn't it?"

"Yes, it is." He wasn't touching his plate, and she said, "Aren't you going to eat your food?"

"I was hungry when I sat down but suddenly I have no appetite," he said. "Not for food."

"Your appetite has gone elsewhere?"

"Oh yes."

"I'm sure you'll get it back. For the right things of course."

Michelle said this last sentence was a playful echo of what she had said when they first met at the graduation, when she said people need pride but for the right things. She said the teasing was enjoyable, but she was worried he might take it in the wrong way. "Do you think this is the right kind of fun?" she asked again.

"What do you think?" I asked.

The session was drawing to a close. "I know people can get upset when teasing goes on too long," she said.

"As long you're aware of what you're doing?"

"Yes, but it's got to end. I can see that."

We stood up and as she left, her buoyant look was gone, replaced with a serious set to her face.

For our next session, Michelle arrived in a light purple pastel ruffle-back strapless taffeta gown with a fitted bodice. She said she was accompanying Jeff to a formal dinner honoring the "higher-ups" in his business. She sat down carefully, folded the ruffle on the left side onto her lap, and took a deep breath.

"So this happened the night after our last session. Jeff invited himself to dinner at my apartment. After dinner, he put the dishes in the sink and reached out for my hands, just like he did before. He said, 'Here? Now?' You remember that's what I said to him the first night he came over?"

"Yes, I do."

"So I said, 'yes, yes.' And then we sort of waltzed into the bedroom and then it was like we just melted into each other. You were right all this time, what I needed was the right partner." She smoothed the dress over again and folded the ruffles. "I guess it's okay that I'm still nervous about it. Even though it really was great, I think I missed some of what it could have been. I think someday soon I could just love it." Michelle laughed and said, "In fact, maybe I won't be able to get enough of it."

During that first episode of making love, she said Jeff was very gentle. But afterward he was so excited that he jumped up on the bed and beat his chest and crowed.

"I started laughing with him, and then we jumped up and down on the bed together. That was so much fun. He makes sex fun."

I looked at her. She broke into a wide grin and said, "Hah, hah, I know what you would say."

"What would I say?"

"We make sex fun together."

"Hmm, now that you mention it, I think that would be a good thing to say."

I noticed there was a new sound to Michelle's laugh. Her "hoot" was now closer to a long purr. It still came from the throat, but there was no harshness to it. After she stopped laughing, she straightened the ruffles once again, shook her bare shoulders back and forth from side to side, and bit her lip.

"Something else troubles you?"

"After the first time, after all the jumping up and down, as soon as he started to go to sleep, I went into the bathroom and I cried."

"You did? How come?"

"It was all the pain from the past. All the times I didn't like sex and I was so lonely and scared. Those times just came flooding back and I couldn't help myself. I just cried and cried, and then when I got back to bed, he was asleep. Do you think it's weird that I cried?"

"No, I think that's how our human system works."

"What do you mean?"

"When good things finally happen at last, they can highlight all the pain that we still have with us, from the bad things."

"So it was normal to cry?"

"Don't you think so?"

"Maybe. It makes me think that Jeff will never know that I'm a person who didn't used to like sex. Do you think he needs to know?"

"What do you think is at stake?"

"He'll never know who I was, unless I tell him."

"Does he need to know?"

"Only if I need him to know who I was, where I came from."

"There might come a time for that?"

"Ah, but not yet, huh?'

"You're enjoying yourself now, aren't you?"

"Yes, why not just enjoy myself, right?"

We smiled once again at each other.

"I really, really like you," Michelle said.

"And I really like you."

With these comments, I had the thought Michelle was "touching base," as she now did regularly, with our reassuring connection to each other. Previously, in our early sessions, these opportunities to connect would have led to angry comments meant to protect herself from that same closeness.

"There's more to tell," she said. "There was a second time. I did something I've never done before. I came on to him."

"You did?"

"Yeah. I was the seducer. I got really turned on by it, and then he did something that turned me on more than anything. He held me tight and he talked to me while we did it. He was so tender. I never knew that was what I wanted but when he did it, I started shaking. That was what I was waiting for. It's my biggest turn on."

"How wonderful."

"Yeah. He even told me I'm his seductress." Michelle made the humming noise from her throat. "The next day he came over and I said 'Talk to me again.' He knew what I meant."

We enjoyed the moment together in silence.

"So this is my guy," she said. "At last."

I nodded.

"He's my man."

"The right one?"

"Yep. He's the one I choose."

Chapter Fifteen—Jeff

The Office of Dr. Yoav Zein. Psychotherapy.

Hours By Appointment.

Friday July 20, 2012.

With the July heat, the condenser on the air conditioner in my office thumped on and off regularly. Jeff entered the office with a handkerchief in hand and wiped the sweat from his face. "I feel like a new man," he said as he sat down.

"What happened?" I asked.

"I always knew it could be this good, I mean with a woman." Then he stopped abruptly and said, "Ok, well maybe I didn't really. Maybe I didn't."

I repeated my question. "What happened?"

"I think I'm in shock. The whole world is different. I don't know where to start."

I waited for him to collect his thoughts. He folded the handkerchief and put it in his pocket.

"So you know I've been seeing Michelle and we've had these

dates," he said, "where we've walked all over the city and talked for
hours."

"Yes, you said that."

"We've been filling each other in on everything that's happened in
our lives. Families, school, jobs, the big events of our lives. Then
afterward we usually sit on a bench in the park and kiss for hours. It's
been really intense, the kissing and all, you know? The kissing's great
but I finally decided I'd had enough of that. I just reached the end of
going on with it, not one more day."

"Yes?"

"I decided to make a move and get things going in bed. It's the
most determined I've ever felt in my life."

Jeff said he laughed to himself as he walked through Central Park
to Michelle's apartment over the previous weekend. "I couldn't help
thinking about Mike. Here I am, heading over to a girl's apartment
with one thing in mind, and I'm just as focused on sex as Mike. But
that's all we had in common. I'm going over to make love to the
woman I'm crazy about, and he would have been going over for a
one-shot deal."

Jeff said that when he arrived at Michelle's apartment, he was
soaked in sweat. She was making dinner. When she saw how
uncomfortable he was in his wet clothes, she gave him a washcloth
and a large bath towel to take a shower. "It's the most 'girly'
bathroom I've ever been in," he told me. "Shelves and shelves of
stuff. She's got lotions, loofahs, shampoos, and a whole shelf of these
things called 'bathing necessities.' And there's all these small jars
with labels in languages I don't understand." While he was in the
shower, he was highly aroused as he thought, "This is where she

showers every day."

After cooling off, he was much more comfortable and walked out to eat dinner in his bare feet. Michelle had made a curry with fresh vegetables from the farmer's market near her apartment and served a homemade lemon sorbet for dessert. After the dinner, he got up from the table to put the dishes in the sink and reached out for her.

At this point, Jeff paused in giving me his account of what happened. He looked around my office and it seemed as if he was struggling to find the words to express himself. When he finally spoke, the words came out in a rush. "When I kissed her, it was like I kissed all of her. That's the first total kiss I've ever had. I wasn't just kissing her, it was like I was taking her out of circulation and making her mine."

"A powerful moment," I said.

"Yes, another one of those things I never knew could happen."

After that kiss, he said, they went to the bedroom with their arms around each other's waists. "It was better than I could have imagined," he said, "and it got better every time." Their lovemaking continued passionately several times during the week, he said. "But then something sort of weird happened."

"What was that?"

"We were right in the middle of doing it, and I was completely beyond myself. I mean, I was in another world. I said, 'Michelle, I adore you. I worship you.' It came out like an explosion."

Jeff said the experience of closeness and passion overwhelmed him, and it was a high point of his life.

"That's great," I said. "But you said something weird happened?"

"Afterward, we were lying in bed with our faces touching,

breathing into each other. It was such an amazing moment but very quiet. I don't know why, but I said the same thing again. I adore you Michelle, I worship you. She didn't say anything either time I said it and her face didn't change. Later on, I couldn't stop thinking about why was that?" He added, "Do you think it's crazy to worship another person?"

"It depends on what's involved."

"I mean, I don't think I'm blind," Jeff continued. "I see the side of Michelle that's just an everyday person. She can be touchy, she's got her sore spots, and she's impatient a lot, and when she's tired, she can even be quarrelsome. I know it comes with the territory and I signed up for it."

"Then what is it that you worship about her?"

"You know we have a way we can really cut through all that obstacle stuff. There's something so incredible when we do. We're just there with each other, saying exactly what's on our minds. I'm really me and she's really her. It's so wonderful. That's what I love about us being together. When we do that, I get the feeling that's what life was meant to be."

"How wonderful, Jeff."

"It is. It comes with that awesome feeling I told you about before, the one where I catch on to what my life's been headed for, even if I didn't know it. Being together with another person was always ahead of me, beyond my reach." Again Jeff seemed to be searching for more words and then found what he wanted to say. "I've never been with anyone who can share that with me. I just hope I haven't taken it too far."

"How could you have taken it too far?"

"I guess I'm worried I might be out on a limb, with the worshipping thing. What do you think?"

"Did you know when a man in the Anglican church gets married, he says to his wife I will worship you with my body?"

"No I never heard that. So I'm not the only one, that's good."

He was quiet for a moment, and then he asked, "So what do you think I'm doing about this worshipping thing?"

"From what you've said, it seems to me you're worshipping the capacity for human beings to share their deepest selves. In another time, people would have said you're sharing your souls."

"I like that," Jeff said, "but do you think Michelle worships that too?"

"What do you think?"

"To be honest, I'm not sure about her. I have to say I'm upset she didn't say anything back to me. Maybe I was waiting for her to say it back to me."

"There weren't any signs of that from her?"

"Right. I suppose she has the right not to meet my expectation if she wants to, just like I have that right too. But then I'm pissed at myself. Right then, I didn't ask her why she didn't say anything. I wanted to know, but I didn't do anything about it."

"I see."

"I guess I've got a lot more to learn about what it takes to be with someone. In a way, it all reminds me of what you said to me the first time I came here. You said I had a desire for someone I didn't love. Do you remember?"

"I do."

"I was really hit by what you said. It was upsetting, but I needed to hear it. But now, like I said, everything's changed. I know what it's like to desire someone you love."

"What a change!"

"It is. When I was with Michelle, I didn't hold anything back. I put my whole self on the line with her and not just in bed. It's the first time I've ever done that."

"How great is that?"

"Yeah, it is. My life was upside down before. Now it's right side up and I'm not holding anything back." He took out the handkerchief and wiped his face again, then folded it and put in his pocket. "So I take it you don't think I'm crazy, for not holding anything back?"

"Jeff, I think in life and in love that can be a form of utter madness or the greatest wisdom."

"What do you mean?"

"I think it's naïve and foolish to hold nothing back, or very wise, depending."

"Depending on what?"

"Depending on who is doing it."

"Those are the rules about this love thing, right? It's up to me to make the difference, isn't it?" Jeff said. "It's better like that, isn't it?"

"I think so."

The session had reached an end. At the door, Jeff said, "I do feel like I've caught up to my own life. If I take a risk and I crash, I guess I'll just pick myself up again."

At the next session, on a still very warm but slightly cooler day, Jeff told me he'd been eagerly looking forward to Friday dinner at Michelle's apartment after they had both been busy all week and had barely seen each other.

Jeff said he arrived at her apartment, sweaty and needing to refresh himself. Once again, he showered in her frilly bathroom and then enjoyed her simple dinner of salad, heirloom tomatoes with Balsamic vinegar, and a crusty French bread with butter and herbs. They chatted about work, put the dishes in the sink and "floated" into the bedroom where they spent the evening making love.

"This is so good," Michelle said as she rested in his arms.

"It is!" he said. "I'm glad you don't need to cry."

She turned in his arms and looked at him. "You knew about that?"

"I did."

"Why didn't you say anything?"

"I wanted you to have what you needed."

"God, you're amazing," Michelle said, then kissed his hands one after the other.

I interrupted Jeff's recounting of the events. "What's this about crying?" I asked.

"After the first night we made love, I drifted off. Next thing I came back awake, and I heard her crying in the bathroom. She thought I was asleep. I was lying there in bed, and of course I was really concerned. I thought it might have been something I did. Or maybe something I didn't do. Then I got it. This is different. Michelle's a person who's gone through a lot in her life, just like I have in mine. She'll tell me about this or I'll ask her about it when she's ready. That's got to be part of how we are with each other. I don't have to worry. It's not going to be like it was with my Dad, all silence. There's a time to talk and a time not to talk. I might not know now, but I'll know later."

He continued with his account of the weekend. The heatwave

broke late that night with heavy storms, and then Saturday was cool and clear. Jeff left her apartment in the morning to go back to his own apartment for a change of clothing. He bought a bouquet of flowers, and took them on the train to visit his mother at her assisted living facility. Then in the afternoon, he took the train back, went to his apartment, changed into a suit jacket, and arrived at Michelle's apartment a few minutes late to pick her up for a dinner engagement. But things didn't go as planned. Instead, he got his opportunity to settle his question about "worshipping."

Michelle opened the door to her apartment and said curtly, "I'm not going." When Jeff followed her into the bedroom, he saw Michelle's clothes were thrown on the floor. She sat down on the bed in her underwear. He had been expecting to pick her up, dressed in one of her beautiful outfits, ready for dinner at an upscale restaurant with Ronnie and Ronnie's latest date.

"What's wrong?" he asked.

"I'm so pissed off I could scream."

"What happened?"

Cursing and swearing "better than a sailor," Michelle told him about events from her work. She was spluttering with rage at one of her co-workers who had "dumped" a load of urgent work on Michelle with an unexpected weekend email message. The more she talked, the angrier she got.

"God, I know what a bite this is," he said. He knew how much people at work could make life difficult, he'd been through it. But he was also nervous that Michelle was about to begin rehashing her lengthy story again. Time was passing. Ronnie and her date were waiting for them at the restaurant.

"What would you know about it?" Michelle asked sharply.

"I know a lot about it," he said. Their voices were rising.

"You couldn't give a shit," Michelle yelled. "All you care about is getting to the fucking restaurant on time." She was wild-eyed. "You're like all the rest, you bastard. You're like all the rest. You...are...like...all the rest."

"That's not all I care about," Jeff said. Then he turned and headed for the door.

"Where are you going?"

"I'm leaving. I can't let you say things like that to me."

"You've got your pride," Michelle said sarcastically.

"Yes, I do," Jeff said. "I wanted you to have your pride, too. But not at the expense of mine." He walked to the door and closed it without looking back. He stopped at the elevator and didn't press the down button. He hit both fists on the wall above the buttons. Out loud, he said: "Everything in my life always winds up upside down." And then, "I've got to flip it."

Later, she told him what happened when he left. "I was sitting there on the bed, I was steaming, but I replayed what we just said about pride. Remember that was the first thing we ever said to each other? Everyone needs pride, but not the wrong kind? I thought, oh yeah, I've had the wrong kind of pride lots of times. I was rubbing my arm where I have the scar from where my dog Mimi bit me. I hadn't even heard most of what you'd just said to me. Some of your words just floated back into my mind: 'What a bite this is.' And I thought, a bite? Damn right, I could just bite you. Wait a minute, where was that from? Of course! With Mimi. Even if she bit me, I loved her!"

With these thoughts, Michelle ran in her underwear to the door, opened it, and took a step into the hallway. Jeff was standing at the elevator and he didn't turn around when the door opened.

"Oh, Jeff, I'm so sorry." Weeping, she said, "Don't leave. You'll never have to go through this again. I swear it."

He turned and looked at her. It occurred to him that this was not likely to be true, that they would have arguments in the future, but that was not a reason to leave.

Through her tears, she said, "I worship you, too."

He walked back to her and they hugged in the doorway. Michelle pulled him into the apartment and closed the door. She smiled through the tears that were still flowing, ran to the closet, pulled out a pair of heels and slipped into her dress. They left for the restaurant without saying another word. Later, after a meal in which they held hands under the table, they came back to her apartment and, as they were getting ready for bed, Michelle reached out to Jeff and put her arms around him.

"It scared me when you said that," she said.

"What?"

"It scared me to be worshipped. I was sure I couldn't live up to it. And I felt if I worshipped you, you'd use it against me. But now I know that was all a thing of the past."

She held him tight.

"I love you, Jeff," she said. "Go ahead and worship me with all your heart. I worship you with mine."

Chapter Sixteen—Michelle
The Office of Dr. Grace Brennan.
Hours By Appointment.

Friday, September 7, 2012.

When Michelle returned to our sessions in September after the vacation, she wore a smart butterfly-waist black silk jacket and matching flare pants. She looked relaxed and contented. She wanted to tell me about her vacation trip, two weeks of fishing and camping on the Madison River with Jeff. She said she had been worried about spending that much time together by themselves, but on the trip, there was a very comfortable balance of talk and silence, a first time experience with a man for her. Then she gave me an account of one special day that seemed to last a lifetime.

On the morning before the last night of their trip, eating a breakfast of trout cooked with herbs and the last of their eggs, Jeff put his fork down and said to her, "I've got an idea I want to tell you and I hope you won't laugh."

"Ok, I promise not to laugh," she said.

"Let's marry ourselves here, under the stars." When she didn't respond, he added, "We can have a regular wedding when we get back."

"Oh," she said, "but I have nothing to wear."

"Then let's wear nothing."

She was about to say something but kept quiet. During the afternoon, she wove two rings from prairie grass, and two garlands from small flowers she found growing near their campsite. Having agreed to write their own vows, they spent the last hours of the day apart. When the sun went down, and she sat watching the stars come out across the sky, Jeff came to her and said, "It's time, now."

Wearing only the garlands, they climbed up to a small hilltop overlooking a meadow that was now bathed in shadows. They knelt down together and looked up.

"Put your hand on my heart," Jeff said. He placed her hand on his heart and held it there, with his own hand over hers.

"Michelle, in the presence of these stars and my heart, I take you to be mine and to be yours. I know that loving you today is only a part of what I will know in days to come. We have already started on an adventure of knowing more of love that has beginnings, more and more beginnings. I give thanks to the universe that we are alive at this moment."

She took his hand and placed it on her heart, and covered his hand with both of hers.

"Jeff, I will love you when the sun is down and the moon is up and when the moon is down and the sun is up. When I am awake I will love you and when I am asleep, my heart will be awake to love you. When I give myself to you, I will hold nothing back but my love is my own, I give it freely. My love is my precious gift to you. Wed me to you, and I will wed you to me."

They drank to each other from a plastic bottle filled with water they had filtered from the river. "Our well of living waters," Jeff called it. Then they exchanged the rings she had woven from the grasses around the camp.

After the ceremony, they walked in silence down the hill to their tent. "Our palace?" she said. Jeff picked her up at the threshold of the tent and carried her in. Smiling, after laying her down inside the tent, he stroked her hair and then her face. "More love," he said. "More love," she replied. "More love," he replied. "And more love," she said.

After Michelle finished telling me about her special day, she was silent, relishing the memory to herself. It took some time for both of us to come back to the here and now in my office. Finally, she wiped her eyes and said, "It's amazing, isn't it?"

"Yes it is." I added, "Congratulations."

"Thank you."

We savored the moment for quite some time. Then Michelle asked, "Was it ok to make our own vows?"

"What do you think?"

"I guess I feel nervous about it. Isn't it going against tradition?" She leaned back on the couch and looked at the ceiling of the office, searching for the right words, then she looked down at me. "Wasn't I being presumptuous? What gives me the right to do something like that?"

"Didn't you say you both did it?" I asked.

"We did. So what gives us the right?"

"It's a good question. Yes, what gives you both the right?"

"You sound like you think we were wrong to do it."

"No, not at all. Do you know where the old idea of making vows comes from?"

"Like what nuns or priests do?"

"Yes. It means to make a promise to your god."

"Well, isn't that what Jeff and I did?"

"I think so."

"It's funny. Here I am worried about it, but I think it's the first time in my life I ever actually felt like I was praying."

Then Michelle asked a question that seemed on the surface to switch topics completely, but in fact, there was a subterranean connection that would become clear later.

"Do you think you were my mother in a past life?" she asked.

"What makes you ask?"

"I just wonder."

I didn't respond but waited for her to say more. I had often wondered about that question myself. In my work with Michelle, I had done my best to play the role of the caring mother, but only when needed. If and when the therapeutic work leads that mother to appear within a patient, she becomes my ally. She is the best kind of mother, the one who gives us life and cares for us, then sends us on our way out into the world with the joy of boundless love. Michelle hadn't been given the advantage of an experience of that kind of mother in her childhood home, but a kind fate brought her into my office where something inexplicable, something larger than both of us, "clicked" between us and created the atmosphere where she could thrive.

"You're the mother I never had," she continued. "It all makes me think of my dog Mimi."

"How so?"

"You let me be mad and angry and bite you when I first came here and you could still be there for me. That was just what I needed. You knew I wasn't biting you because I was mean."

"That's true."

"I've realized something with you, and now with Jeff. I don't need to bite anymore."

"That's wonderful."

"Yeah. In fact, if I feel like biting now, I know it comes from an old habit that I really don't need anymore. If I don't stop myself, I know I actually could be mean."

"Michelle, that's a very powerful realization. You're responsible, now that you're aware."

"Yep, I'm doing my best with it, even with my mother and my sisters."

"What's going on with them?"

Michelle said she was planning her "real" wedding for the first week of January at the Bronx Botanical Gardens, with a reception in the terrace garden room. She was pleasantly surprised that her mother yielded, although very reluctantly, to Michelle's request to plan the wedding by herself. Michelle said she initially wanted to do the planning by herself because she was still hurt and angry with her mother.

"All these years, I've never forgiven her for that whole episode with our nasty neighbor," Michelle said. "I still get sick at the memory of that guy putting his hands all over me. My mother never stopped blaming me for what happened. It was all my fault as far as she's concerned. It's almost like she wanted to believe the worst about me. That was so unfair."

But, on thinking it over, Michelle said she decided to include her mother in the wedding planning after all. "I could go on forever, not forgiving her," Michelle said, "or myself. And it felt like, oh no, I could be in danger of being just as much a stuck person as her. That's not how I want to be. So I realized if I forgive her, it's got to be with the way she is, she's not going to change. Anyway, the most important person who has to believe my side of the story is me."

When Michelle changed her mind and asked her mother to be her "wedding consultant," and to come along on planning trips to the gardens, her mother had been teary and at a loss for words. From then on, there was harmonious talk between them and even a sense of having fun together as they chose the colors of the tablecloths and the napkins and the flower arrangements.

"Then we started to have a fight because I wanted to get a once-used dress and pay for it myself," Michelle said. "She wanted to pay for a designer from Paris to fly over and design a gown for me. It would have cost tens of thousands. So ridiculous."

"How did you handle it?"

"You know how I always call her 'Mother?' So for once, I called her 'Mom.' We were in her bedroom, and I said, 'Mom, I know you want me to have a really special day. This is your way of showing it. I know that, I really do. I want something even more from you. I want you to be my Mom, standing next to me when I get married. I want you to stand next to me whenever I need you. That's what I want. That's what's important to me, more important than my dress. More important than anything. Let's not fight. Let's love each other."

"My gosh, Michelle. That was something," I said.

"Yeah, I guess it was. My mother sat down on a little brocade

footstool in her room and put her head in her hands and cried like a
baby. I put my arms around her. I kissed her head. She said, 'I know I
haven't always been the best mother to you Michelle. I know I
haven't the right to ask you for things. But I want so much for us to
have what you said.'"

Michelle said she rested her head on her mother's shoulder, and
couldn't think of anything to say. Then her mother said, "you'll
always be my baby, but I know Jeff is getting a woman."

I was deeply moved by this moment between Michelle and her
mother. "Michelle," I said, "what a beautiful compliment."

"Yes. For once I feel like my mother appreciates me. It hurts and it
feels so good all at the same time." Michelle reached for a Kleenex
and dabbed her eyes and continued her story.

"So my mother and I went to the bridal boutique, and I tried on a
lot of dresses, and then we both loved this mermaid silhouette with an
off-white lace overlay. It's strapless. I'll wear a little bolero because it
might be cold. The great thing is, I can dance in it."

She sighed and put the tissue in her purse.

"My mother and I have a secret smile now. My sisters picked up
on it right away. There's so much jealousy in my family. There's
never enough love to go around. After one of the fittings, we came
back to the house and everyone was there. We were all sitting in the
living room and then I went into the kitchen by myself. Beth followed
me in, and said, 'What's going on with you and Mother?' I got her
vibe right away, it was very hostile. I did what I usually do. I tried to
put her off the trail."

"What does putting her off the trail mean?" I asked.

"I said to Beth, 'Mom's just relieved she's finally marrying the last one off.' Beth sort of snorted and said, 'She probably thought it would never happen.' And I said 'I gave her a lot of reasons to think so, didn't I?'"

"So you put Beth off the trail of jealousy by putting yourself down?"

"That's how I always did it. That would usually be enough to satisfy her. We were going to leave it there, but then I looked at Beth and it was like I had x-ray vision. What made her so jealous even of a little smile from Mom? Then it hit me, my sister is starving for appreciation, she thinks nobody sees she's special, she's desperate to be included whenever there's love, but she doesn't have a clue how to get what she wants. What a sad way to live. It's tragic for her. When I saw that about her, when I saw what's inside her, I said to her, 'Beth, nobody can take your place in Mom's heart. Or mine. You'll always be my big sister and I'll always love you.' She started to cry, she actually started shaking, and we hugged each other."

"Michelle!"

"Yeah, it's like I have a new family. These people were out to get me, they tore me down, and now I know how to build them up and how to build myself up. It's amazing. They're my dogs."

"Your dogs?"

"Yep, and you know I don't mean anything bad by it. You know how much I loved my dog. Well, I finally saw it, my family are my dogs. They need to be treated that way. You have to pet them, and feed them, and take them out for walks. That's the way you have to love them."

"What does that mean?"

"My parents and my sisters, they're not capable of telling you what they're feeling, and they can't tell you what they need. You have to guess what they need. If you guess right, they get all happy and warm. But only then. Thank goodness it's not like that with my Jeff. We can talk to each other, we can tell each other things, we don't have to guess all the time. We can ask each other for what we want, but not them, no way. So when you realize they're dogs, and you treat them like a dog you love, everything goes right."

"So it is a kind of love?"

"Right, it is. Not the kind of love I have with Jeff. But it's still love. It only goes wrong with my dog family when I act like I still have to be one of them."

"When is that?"

"When I don't know myself what I need, and I want them to do the guessing for me. When I want them to go first, and they don't and they can't. Then I feel that old awful resentment. I just burn with it."

"You burn?"

"Yeah, I used to get so mad I could explode. Why does it always have to be me who makes the first move? That sucked so much when I was growing up. But now I know they haven't got the tools for being first and reaching out to me, so there's no point in getting all wounded about it. But I don't need them to do that anymore. They can be who they are."

With this new perspective on her family, for the next few months of our sessions Michelle told me of the challenging events leading up to her wedding, including the usual slights and tiffs among her relatives, and even among some of the guests. Problems arose because many people couldn't be seated next to each other, particularly among the political and business associates of her parents, many of whom

Michelle had never even met. Michelle called it her "family dog wedding," with special care needed for those that hadn't been "housetrained."

She said it was a completely different story with Jeff's family. Jeff's mother had been ill, but she was well enough to participate in the wedding. She hosted a small "engagement" dinner at a trendy health food restaurant in Manhattan that was a favorite of Michelle's and Jeff's. Before the dinner, she gave Michelle several of the most treasured pieces of her family jewelry, and told Michelle in private that she was the only girl Jeff ever brought home that she truly liked. In the lead-up to the wedding, Jeff's small group of relatives were the best behaved of everyone, and Michelle found it a relief to spend time with them. It was an even greater relief when the wedding went off without a hitch, although several of her relatives drank too much and made embarrassing speeches.

As for the wedding gifts, she and Jeff had asked for none to be given. Instead, their invitations included a list of their favorite charities, for anyone who wanted to make a donation in their honor. Late at night after the excitement of the wedding, sitting on the bed in her apartment, they opened a large white velvet drawstring bag, stuffed with dozens of cards from the guests. Michelle's mother had given them the bag, and there was an envelope with a card taped securely to the bag's side. Inside the envelope was an exquisite card with a short note inside, signed by both of her parents. The note said they wanted Jeff and Michelle to accept "a gift from our hearts." The gift was a large check, and the note said the money was for them to rent a new apartment they could move into as newlyweds, and to buy furniture to suit their taste.

Michelle threw the card down on the floor and said, "That's so typical. Money. That's what they have to give." She said she was "opposed to the whole crummy idea."

"Maybe we should talk about it," Jeff said. He picked up the card from the floor.

"There's nothing to talk about," Michelle said. "I know why they're doing it."

"You do?"

"Of course I do. You don't know a thing about it."

"Maybe I know a lot about it," he said.

"You are just like..." At that moment, she stopped herself. She was about to argue more intensely, to say things she didn't mean, to accuse Jeff of being "like all the rest," but once again she played back his words. They were so familiar. "I know a lot about it." Those were the same words he used before their first quarrel.

"Okay, okay. What do you know about it?" she asked.

"Are you afraid of what it will mean?" he asked. "If you take the money from them?"

"You're damn right," she said.

"Don't you think this is their way of trying to connect to us? Ok, so money is the only way they do it, they don't give hugs or say nice things. But isn't that the best they know how to do?"

"Maybe. Probably."

"Anyway, do you really need to worry about why they're doing it? Aren't you already doing what you need to do, to make your own life?"

"Maybe. Probably."

Then he said, "So do you really need to fight them?"

"Okay, probably not."

"Then why not let them feel like they're doing something good for us?" He waited for her response, but she didn't say anything. He added, "They might never know it, but if we accept the check, it would be our gift to them too."

Michelle stuck out her tongue but gave a slight smile. He said, "Hey, I know you resent things about them, and for damned good reasons. I'm not suggesting you give up the right to feel that way."

"But it's a control game," Michelle said. "If we take the check, they'll think they've won. We'll be obligated to do what they want with it. That's how they always do it, it's always about what they want. With them, everything comes with strings attached. I don't want to be controlled by what they want."

"Then let's just not play in the control game," he said. "Let's cut the strings."

"How do we do that?"

"If we're grateful for their gift, it doesn't have to mean we're giving in. Being grateful doesn't mean you need to feel obligated to them, and neither do I. Aren't we the ones in control of our lives?"

She smiled again.

"Hey, isn't it always up to us to decide what we do with our money?" he asked. After a few moments passed, again he said, "We're in this together, aren't we?"

"We are," she said. With that, the urge to fight, and the urge to bite, evaporated. She added, "We definitely are, my man."

As Michelle finished her account of their conversation, she shook her head and said, "Isn't he something?"

"He is," I said.

She said the talk with Jeff about the gift from her parents, and the closeness that came from working something out together, filled her with happiness. Again, she said, "He's really something isn't he?"

"I think so."

"I've really been admiring the way my parents are taking to him. He's training them," she said, laughing. "He's a damned good dog trainer. And then when he turns it on me, I know when he's doing it, but it works just the same."

Chapter Seventeen—Jeff

The Office of Dr. Yoav Zein. Psychotherapy.

Hours By Appointment.

Friday May 3, 2013.

It was spring again, the white dogwood was in bloom in Central Park, and a mood of expectation seemed to hover over the city. Before my patients came in the morning, I opened the windows wide to enjoy the fresh air, as I liked to do. The buoyancy in the air seemed to match Jeff's mood.

"One of the most amazing things happened yesterday," he said. "I took the day off from work just to be with Michelle in this beautiful weather. We were holding hands, walking down Broadway in the Eighties, just after lunch, and I was having that magical feeling again like we were walking in the enchanted city. You remember I told you about that feeling before?"

"Yes I remember."

"We were just strolling along, and then who do we run into? It's Mike. Completely out of the blue, after so long, I saw him half a block away, walking toward me. He was on his way to the old bar, the one where we all used to hang out."

Jeff said he and Mike were both wearing light brown suits with vertical striped shirts, which reminded him of how they often shared clothing when they were roommates in college. Mike smiled for a brief moment when he recognized Jeff from among the crowd of people on the sidewalk, then a scowl came over Mike's face. As they approached each other, Jeff reached out to shake Mike's hand, but Mike punched him in the arm.

"Hey, asshole," Mike said.

"Hi Mike, how are you?"

"Like you give a crap."

"Ok, want to start again?"

"No, but let's get a drink."

Jeff ignored the comment and put his arm around Michelle. "Michelle, I want to introduce you to my friend Mike. Mike, this is my wife, Michelle."

"Ah, the famous wife," Mike said. He looked her up and down as he shook her hand. "You are enchanting. What makes him think he deserves you?"

"And you are the infamous Mike," she said in a derisive tone.

Jeff stopped telling me his story, smiled, and said, "I know that tone of voice of hers so well. You can't miss the message. She means 'get lost, jerk.' Michelle is nobody to mess with." He added, "I didn't need her to defend me but it seemed like she wanted to, and that was really sweet. I've never been with any woman who did that before." Jeff continued with his account of what happened:

Mike held onto Michelle's hand but she pulled her hand away.

Mike bowed mockingly.

"Don't think I haven't heard about you," Michelle said, in the same tone of voice.

"All of it bad, but all of it true, I'm sure," Mike said. He added, "May I have the honor of buying you a drink too?"

Michelle ignored him and turned to Jeff and said, "Honey, I've got my errands to run, and I'm sure you've got a lot to talk about. I'll meet you back home for dinner." She kissed Jeff, gave a short nod to Mike, and walked off. Mike continued looking after her but she didn't turn around.

"All right, let's go," Jeff said. Once they were inside the bar, they sat down in a booth, and there was an awkward silence while they waited for the barmaid. While Mike was looking for her, Jeff saw that Mike's face was puffier than before, with small spider veins around his eyes and mouth. When Mike turned back, Jeff glanced away quickly and took a closer look at the place where they had spent so much time together in college. The bar was dark, paneled with strips of stained wood, with long black painted beams across the ceiling. A framed mirror on the wall ran the same length as the bar's counter, and the round rotating red-cushioned stools were worn and cracked, just as they had been when Jeff was a student. The bar was nearly deserted. The waitress appeared, she was college age, with a dirty apron but an efficient air.

"You could be the love of my life," Mike said to her. He looked around, gestured to the rest of the bar, and said, "My darling, it's not busy. Can I buy you a drink so you can sit with us for a while?"

"No, and don't you remember what I told you the last time you were here? The boss doesn't allow us to sit with customers."

"The last time we spoke is something I can never forget, it haunts me. Say you'll go out with me, and my whole life will change."

Ignoring Mike, she said, "Beers, gentlemen?"

"Too early for me. I'll have a ginger ale," Jeff said.

"A Scotch on the rocks for me and some rocks for my friend here. He hasn't got any."

Jeff stopped telling me his story and said, "Mike seemed angrier than before, and I was wondering if the anger was mostly about me, or maybe not. I mean, he was definitely trying to get a rise out of me, but I was having such a great day, it didn't bother me at all. I wondered if he was pissed off because of what happened between us, or is this just him, angry all the time? So I just ignored what he said and asked him how he was doing." Jeff continued with Mike's response:

"Same old, same old," Mike said. "Same job. I was fired, but they took me back. I'm not gonna ask how you're doing. Mr. Success, I'm sure."

"You sound bitter, Mike."

"Oh, here's Mr. Psychologist. I suppose next you're gonna recommend therapy for me like you did for Noel."

"You're mistaken. I never recommended therapy for Noel."

"Sure you did. She's been in it ever since you kicked her out of your sleeping bag."

"You know about that?"

"She told me about it after the divorce," Mike said. The drinks arrived, and he finished his Scotch in one gulp and ordered another. "So how come you didn't tell me? You were supposed to be my best friend. Some friend. What kind of a friend keeps something like that to himself?"

At that moment, Jeff stopped recounting what had happened and looked at me, shaking his head. "That whole magical feeling I'd had?" he said. "It just evaporated like a flash. I felt awful, really guilty, like I'd let him down."

"What did you say?" I asked.

"I was just in shock. For a while, I didn't say anything," Jeff said, "I just let him go on with what he had to say. I was having that old upside-down feeling I've told you about."

"Yes?"

"It was like my life turned upside again. All along, I've been thinking about Mike's shortcomings and how I don't want to be like him. I'm not saying that was a mistake, there was a lot to learn about that, but now I was blown away because I saw Mike was looking at me the same way, he saw my shortcomings, and he wasn't wrong. It was a really painful moment for me."

"That was a difficult realization."

"It really was. I was feeling awful, thinking about how many nasty surprises there are in life, and Mike was just going on talking, really angry. But now I didn't blame him for being angry."

"What did he say?"

Again Jeff continued his account of their conversation:

"To this day, I don't get it," Mike said. "Everybody knows you had the hots for her, and then when you get the golden opportunity, you don't do it? What were you thinking? Don't even try to sell me some noble crap about how you were being loyal to me."

"You're right," Jeff said, ignoring Mike's last question. "I should've told you. Even if you and I weren't talking, I should've found a way. I screwed up. I'm sorry Mike, I wasn't being a good friend. I really regret that."

"All right," Mike said. His mood seemed to evaporate too, his face softened, and after a pause, he said, "Look, no worries, kid. It's ancient history now, water under the bridge. But I still don't get why you didn't do it with her."

"You might not believe this, but I didn't know myself. That's a big part of why I got into therapy, to try and find out."

"I don't know why I've done a lot of things myself," Mike said. He turned and looked for the waitress, impatient for his next drink. He turned back to Jeff and said, "I talked to Noel a couple of months ago, and she said therapy's the best thing that ever happened to her. She might be right. She's a lot happier than she was with me anyway."

"Wow, I'm happy for her. I'm really glad to hear that."

"Well, you can take the credit."

"I told you, I didn't recommend therapy for Noel. She must have found it on her own."

"Ok, keep up the lie, see if I care." Mike took off his suit jacket and laid it across the back of the booth. "So you finally got hitched. Happily married. How do you do it? If I don't get some new tail every week I go crazy."

"They say married men get more sex than single men."

"I can believe it. You don't have to work at it as much as I do. Nobody has any idea how much work I have to do just to get laid."

"I never looked at it that way."

"No, you wouldn't, would you?" Mike's new drink arrived and he quickly took his glass, drank it down, put the empty glass back on the barmaid's tray, and ordered a third Scotch. His face had turned redder, and he was talking more slowly. The angry tone was completely gone, and he asked in a wistful tone, "So what's the secret to a happy marriage?" He added, "I certainly screwed up mine."

"I don't have the secret," Jeff said.

"You know I could always tell when you were bullshitting me. You do have the secret. You just don't want to tell me."

"Ok, maybe I have some idea, but I don't claim to be an expert."

"So go ahead, lay it on me."

"I don't really know. Maybe I just sort of found out what works for me."

Mike frowned and shook his head.

"Ok," Jeff said, "Here's what I found out. I had to raise my bar about everything. Sex, women, myself."

"What does that mean?"

"It means I was stuck, and I didn't see what was behind it."

"Behind what?"

"Behind being stuck, behind everything always going wrong for me. I was driven. But not like you. I never seemed to get what I wanted."

"You think I always get what I want? You really don't know me, do you? It's more like I never get what I want."

"What do you mean?"

"It's never that great. I've been with so many women I'd need a ten-year calendar and a calculator to know how many. It always seems like the next one could be the one. The one where I finally get whatever the hell it is I'm going for. But it never is. At this point, I don't expect it ever will be."

"So you need to raise your bar too."

"Where did you get that? And what the hell does it mean?"

"Actually, I got it for the first time from the fish."

"What are you talking about?"

"I was lying in my sleeping bag in the morning on that last trip. You and everybody else were all downstream. Or so I thought."

"That makes two of us. I thought Noel was right behind us in another canoe."

There was an awkward moment. "Yeah, I guess we were both wrong," Jeff said.

"Yeah, well, like I said that's in the past," Mike said. "So you were lying there?"

"I was. I was thinking about salmon and how they swim upstream to spawn. It's not natural. I mean, of course it's natural because it's nature, but there's something about it that hit me. They're willing to go against the flow to get what they want, and they make a huge effort to get it. And I thought, what about me?"

"So now you're taking life lessons from fish?"

Jeff threw up his hands in mock exasperation.

Mike laughed and said, "Ok, Mr. Philosopher, raising the bar means exactly what?"

"It means I was missing something. I was meant to go for more. More than just what having sex with any available woman can offer."

"There isn't anything more. Believe me, I've tried it."

"Oh yes there is. That's the secret. There is more, a lot more."

"So how do you get that 'more' you're talking about, not that I really believe you."

"You've got to work to become more of the person you were meant to be."

"That sounds like such a crock."

"Well, you asked me," Jeff said. With that, he threw up his hands again. This time he turned his head, saw his upraised hands in the long mirror of the bar, and stopped at the sight of himself. Did the gesture mean he was giving up again on Mike and their friendship? He turned back. "Mike, I don't buy it," he said. "I don't believe you have to push away everything that could help you. I just don't buy it."

Mike looked surprised. "Whoa, that's the old Jeff we know and love. Ok, ok. More of a person. Why?"

"Because you can't make it work with another person, with a woman, until you know more about yourself. You can't deal with things in another person if you can't handle what's driving you. And that's why you've got to raise the bar about how you deal with yourself."

"So give me an example of how you raised the bar."

"I stopped chasing after things that don't have much to offer."

"Hah. So you're finished with the chase?"

"I'm finished with chasing after illusions about myself and women. I'm not a prisoner of that anymore. I think that's why it didn't work out for me a lot of times. I wasn't meant to be a prisoner."

"So you think I'm a prisoner?"

"You said it, not me."

"You could be right. I can't say that chasing women has brought me anything very grand in life." Mike jiggled the ice in his glass. "I suppose I would stop if there was anything better."

"Maybe it's not really women that have been disappointing you."

"Then what is it, swami, pray tell?"

"It's that you're trying to find out something about yourself."

"Is that what you really think?"

"Yes, I really do."

At that, Mike straightened up and said, "A few days ago, I saw you and your wife walking down the quad. You had your arms around each other's waists and you were laughing. And I thought, she must be the woman. She's the one I want, she's the one I've been looking for all this time. I was fired up. And then I had such a pain. It went right through me. It's something I always feel when I see a guy with a woman who looks like she's the one for him. It's like that guy found it but I didn't. I haven't. And then all of a sudden, the pain just disappeared and I felt something I never felt before. I thought, Jeff and Michelle, you guys, you'll find it, the thing I was looking for. At least somebody will find it. It'll be found. So I don't have to do it. I can relax. As long as somebody finds it, that's good enough. It's taken care of, and that's all that's needed. I never felt so free in all my life. And then who do I run into today? You."

"That's amazing."

"Since then I've been thinking I need to figure out if I can reinvent myself. Maybe that's why I ran into you."

"Well, I think it's possible to reinvent yourself. I know because I did it. But it's a long story. I could tell you if you're really interested."

"What makes you think I'm not interested?"

"I'm not an idiot."

"No, you're not. And you were the only person who ever bothered to talk to me as if I wasn't an idiot. I'll always be grateful for that."

"I'm kind of blown away. I never knew that about you."

"You really think I'm a bad guy, don't you?"

"No, Mike, I don't. I really don't. But I do think you're missing something."

"Like I said, you could be right." He looked at his empty glass. "I'm missing my next Scotch."

At this point, Jeff hadn't finished his recounting of the story of meeting Mike, but we had reached the end of the session. We agreed to continue next time and as we shook hands at the door, he said, "Meeting up with Mike was another one of those zingers I get in life. This one was about friendship. And I thought love was the only thing I wasn't ready for."

Chapter Eighteen—Michelle
The Office of Dr. Grace Brennan.
Hours By Appointment.

Friday, May 3, 2013.

When Michelle entered the office, she noticed me looking at a small antique-style ruby pin in the lapel of her one-button black silk business suit. "It's a gift from Jeff's mother," she said, "she put it on me in her bedroom and then she hugged me." As she sat down, she ran her finger over the pin and pulled up the collar to look at it, then she frowned.

"Something bothers you?" I asked.

"Yes, this pin scares me."

"It does? Why is that?"

"It reminds me of this quote I read somewhere. 'When a child doesn't receive love, he can seldom give it later.'"

"Does that worry you about Jeff?"

"I'm worried about it for both of us and for the universe."

"What do you mean?"

"This isn't just any old pin," she said. "Jeff's family history is in this pin. It belonged to Jeff's great-great-grandmother. The story is she always wore this pin on all her clothes, it was given to her by her husband as a wedding gift. Everybody knew she always wore it. But when her son got married, she took her new daughter-in-law into her own bedroom, sat her down on the very bed her son was born in, took off the pin, and put it on the girl's blouse. That shocked everybody. It was an amazing gift, welcoming the new bride into the family. To make a gesture like that was something pretty special. I think it was one of those things real mothers do."

"Oh, yes," I said.

"So that started a family tradition," Michelle said. "In all the next generations, the mothers handed down the pin to their daughters-in-law, and now Jeff's mother gave it to me. It gives me chills. If I have a son, I'll give it to his wife."

"What a beautiful history."

"It is. This pin has stitched together the women in Jeff's family, crossing back and forth. It means so much to me, like I have something from the women in his family going way back."

"That's great, but a moment ago you said the pin scares you. Why is that?"

"There's a whole bunch of reasons. You should've seen my sisters when they heard the story about the pin. They were so angry they were ready to claw at me. They're jealous because they're both in a cold war with their husbands' mothers. It's a fight for control and it never ends. And when my own mother heard about it, she gave me a look that would freeze the blood in your veins." Michelle ran her finger over the pin and pulled the collar up to look at it again, and then she frowned again. "So you want to know what really scares me about it? I'll tell you. Don't you think you need to have the family behind you in order to make a marriage work?"

"What do you think?"

"It's why I'm scared. My family, they're not behind me, even with all the new things I've been doing to make things work with them. Look at how they went and got so mean and cold about a little pin. And Jeff's mother is sweet as can be, but Jeff says he can't get over how different we are from his parents."

"Because?"

"Because his parents never talked to each other. They had a lot of silence in their marriage. And they never talked to their son either. When I wear this pin, I wonder if it's realistic to hope Jeff and I can keep up a marriage, I mean a good marriage. Look at where we come from. I'm scared because I feel like, with no family to back us up, we're taking a big risk."

I waited to see if Michelle would arrive at answers to her own questions.

"It's not like there's just one person in my family who's the problem. I come from a family that's a whopping big mess. The missing love in my family is like a bottomless pit and I used to fall into that hole all the time. When I look at Jeff and me, I have to say we're both beginners, neither one of us knows how to make a good marriage. We're starting from scratch." She looked straight ahead. "Shouldn't I be scared?"

"Should you?"

"What if our love isn't strong enough to last?"

"That's a fear that can paralyze."

"Oh God, you're so right. I mean, what if we do our best with what we've got, what if we really try hard, but it isn't enough? Isn't that possible?"

"You know it's possible, don't you?"

"I do and it's so painful. I can see now how my family did their best. I really do see that. But it just wasn't good enough. What right do I have to think I'm any different?"

Again, I waited to see if Michelle would answer her own question.

"Yes, it could all end," she said. Tears formed in her eyes and she said in the most plaintive voice, "I don't want to lose it all." After wiping her eyes, she asked, "What do you think?"

"Haven't we talked about how fears are a message?"

"We have. But what kind of message?"

"Is the fear that you're just like your family?"

"That's right."

"How might you be different?"

"Well, for one thing, I'm actually worried about love, and I'm worried about what I don't know about it. My family, they're not."

"That's a good start, isn't it?"

"It better be. Nobody in my family focuses on love. It's not number one for them, it's not even on the list. They're all busy trying to prove something, or to get back at somebody, or one-up somebody. They're going after some big crazy ambition for something they don't need, and you can't talk to them because they have their wounded pride. Last weekend the whole family spent the night at my parent's house, and I walked into the living room in the morning, and I saw Beth. I was still sleepy, and I said, 'oh, your hair looks nice,' and she was offended. I mean, she was outraged and she yelled at me. She said, 'I knew all along you didn't like my hair. I knew you were lying before.' She actually called me a liar to my face. With my family, even a little compliment gets twisted into criticism."

"What a difficult situation."

"Yeah, they twist everything and they're just so angry all the time."

"Well, even if you're also angry at times, aren't you different because you can focus on other things?"

"Can I?"

"Yes. We know you have your pride and your anger too, just like them, but how many times have we talked about serving the love you and Jeff actually have? That's a real departure from your family, isn't it?"

"Are you saying because I can do that, I don't have to be so scared?"

"I think so. If you strengthen how you serve the love, you can overcome a lot of the fear."

"It's amazing you said that. This week I was with Jeff in my apartment and we were just hanging out and not saying anything, he was reading and I was doing some needlepoint, and I realized it wasn't a bad kind of silence at all. I thought, here I am with my man, and it's so good just being together. I was just loving him while we were quiet, and it was heaven. All of a sudden, I wondered where did the fear go? Then it came to me that the time I get worried is when I'm not with Jeff and my thoughts run away with me. If I stay connected to him and what we have between us, then I'm fine."

Michelle got up and walked to the window and looked out on the traffic on Lexington Avenue. Then she turned and looked around the room as if taking it in for the first time.

"You're connected to that kind of love, aren't you?"

"I am."

Michelle sighed. "It all makes me wonder if there's a god of love."

"That's a big one! Can you say more?"

"To be perfectly honest, for a long time I didn't believe a lot of things you said. Like you said sex could be uplifting if you were with the right person. I thought that was such a crock. I thought you were full of it. I actually laughed at you in the elevator after that session."

"I see."

"Then I found out you were right. When you make love with the right person, it feels like you're creating the world all over again."

"Oh Michelle, that's so wonderful."

"It really is. Considering where I started. You know how turned off I was."

"Yes."

She straightened her collar and patted the pin and looked at me with that direct gaze that so often in the past had anger in it. Now there was only the slightest flicker of annoyance. "And even right from the beginning, you were the only one that could see that I could love. Nobody else could see it. I was wondering how you could do all that, and then I thought, she must know about the god of love."

I waited for her to say more.

"You knew what to do here. I mean about love. And you knew what Jeff and I were doing, when we made our vows on the top of the mountain. Remember? Didn't we make our vows to the god of love?"

"Yes, I think you did."

"So I was thinking, if there's a god of love, maybe you can rely on that, if you can't rely on what you got from your family, right?"

"Don't you think so?" I asked.

Michelle didn't answer. We paused and there was a long silence. I thought I heard the bell of a nearby church. At that moment, an eerie sensation came over me, as if something momentous was about to happen. It was a feeling I've had in my work whenever crucial moments were about to occur. I shivered, and somehow I knew something very important was about to happen.

"May I call you Grace?" Michelle asked.

"Yes, certainly."

"Grace, the thing I learned from coming here is you don't have to be stuck with what you didn't get. I learned that here."

There it was. The defining moment of all our work together, in a simple statement that encapsulated a long journey. A great yet quiet moment of victory had occurred. At that, Michelle went to the walnut table where I kept the many things from my travels. She picked up a large glass paperweight with red roses and smoothed her hands over the top. "People who don't know about the god of love are only half alive. Like I was. Don't you think?"

"Yes, if you want to come alive in this life, you must know there is something so much greater about love. It's beyond words."

"You know, before I came to see you, I would've thought that was the most ridiculous thing I'd ever heard."

"And now?"

"Now my life is about love. I want to know everything there is to know about it."

"That's a beautiful thing, isn't it?"

"Yes it is. I guess there are some people who are lucky and get love handed down, in the family, right?"

"Yes, but it's never something that can be handed down entirely or completely. There's always something new that has to be added to it."

Michelle brightened as she sat down again and said, "That's just what I was looking for. Now I feel better about the half-way kind of love I got in my family. Maybe the good thing is, it leaves something for me and Jeff to add on. Something that's new."

Once again, we shared what Michelle called a "secret smile." There was another moment of silence, and then she continued. "It's so strange. You remember how Jeff and I had this big misunderstanding about worshipping love? If we hadn't misunderstood each other about worshipping love, we wouldn't have the closeness we have now. It's kind of like that sealed the union. But only because we got over the misunderstanding," she said. She put down the paperweight on the table next to the couch. "It's like, things going wrong can give you the chance to correct things. That's something I never knew. It's the same with my first wedding dress," she said.

"Wait, I'm confused. What was your first wedding dress?"

"My skin." She laughed that purring laugh. "Not exactly what every girl dreams of," she said, "but a major breakthrough for me."

"What do you mean?"

"When we were on our camping trip, and Jeff asked me to marry him under the stars, and said we could have an 'official' wedding when we got back, and I said I didn't have any clothes, for just a second I was going to say no to him. You know how much I wanted to be a bride. At first it seemed like such a disappointment, that's not how I dreamed my wedding would be."

"At first?"

"Yeah, I felt really mad. Like he was trying to take something away from me. I started to get ready to get back at him. You know, start yelling. I got all charged up. How could he do that? So thoughtless. So disconnected. I was ready to start biting him. And then it all went poof! Like popping a balloon."

"What happened?"

"I thought, I could really mess this up. If I decide that's what I'm going to do, no one can stop me. I have the power and I have the freedom. I can do whatever I want. Right then, I realized I have the power to ruin a relationship, just like my family."

"It is a kind of power for sure."

"So I didn't say anything back when he asked me to get married that night, and he was waiting. I thought, ok, I'm not going to ruin things. But if I don't tell him how mad and disappointed I am, what can I do? I can't just sit with it. I'll go crazy if I do."

"Yes, what could you do?"

"Then I remembered what you said about the rules of the game. When he advances, you lose your chance for the entire rest of the game unless you cross over, en passant. Ok, I thought, this is the game of love? Love is a game with a lot at stake. It's for real. Ok, I said to myself, Michelle, get in there and do your best, dammit. Don't let it pass you by. Play the game, play the game of love and see what happens."

"So you got yourself into the game?"

"I did." After a pause, she continued, "I found out what having a partner does for me."

"What does it do for you?"

"Before I came here, everything everybody did seemed like it was wounding me. That was because I only looked at things through my eyes. After I came here, I started looking at myself through other people's eyes."

"What do you mean?"

"I never told you this. One day after a session with you, I took a good hard look at myself and I wondered, where does all this pride and anger and hurt come from? I didn't make it up from nothing. And I can't blame it all on my family, even if they're worse than a lot of others. They're kind of extreme, they've got their pride, pride, pride. But they didn't make it up from nothing either. So where is it all coming from? I was on the trail of something here and it took me so long to get going on it."

"It seemed like a very long time to you?"

"It did. Remember when I was a receptionist and I was so bored at work? After I started coming to see you, I was fighting with myself about this awful wounded pride thing. I spent all day doing that, I was lucky I didn't have to pay attention to anything else."

"You needed time for that."

"I did. Remember how I was so bored I used to scream?"

"Oh yes, I remember."

"Was I ever a whopping big mess. I'm so sorry you had to listen to me. So there I was at work, answering the phone, ok let's be real, I wasn't answering the phone half the time, and nobody could see I was on the rack. The person I was really annoyed with was me, and I was in agony because it was getting stronger and stronger all the time, and it seemed like it would never stop. Nobody could see it was building up to something fierce. But you saw the agony."

"I did."

"For a long time I was really mad at you. I thought you were so cruel. Here I'm in agony, you see me in agony, and you don't do anything? You see I'm roasting in my own fire? I thought, she better be damn sure that's the only way."

"Yes."

"When I finally looked at myself, as if I was watching myself through your eyes and through the eyes of everyone else, it hit me. I did it to myself. I… did… it… all… to… myself. I made myself bored, I made myself angry, I made myself so resentful my family called me Michelle R., I made myself go with guys who ignored me, I made myself have sex when I didn't want to, I made myself lonely and miserable. Oooh, it hurt so much to face that. I just roasted in that fire. And you just let me. You let me roast. You let me burn."

"Yes."

"I thought you were so cruel. I was always wondering, isn't there another way? Did it really have to be that way?"

I was silent.

"All I know is I got burned all the way down to the ashes. It burned away the old me."

"That was necessary after all, wasn't it?"

"I guess so. When you didn't try to save me I was sure you were abandoning me. I was sure you were just a crazy bitch. And in the middle of that, when I was so scorched I didn't even have the energy to give up, when I felt like I was just roasted down to nothing, what came over me? Hope, like I never felt before. That's when the boredom went poof, and that's when something in me started to change."

"Oh yes."

"And after I was burned down to the ashes, I got to know how much power I have. Bad and good. Like I said, I can ruin a relationship. I mean really destroy it, burn it to the ground. I could do it, and I can do it. I can just go crazy when I feel like I'm being wounded. For a long time, I wanted to do that with you, I wanted to burn you back. I wanted to yell and scream at you. But some little voice told me, she must be letting you burn because she thinks you need it. Maybe you even wanted to stop me from roasting sometimes? Didn't you?"

"Oh yes, Michelle. There were a few moments when I was really on the fence."

"But I finally saw you were staying right with me. You knew about the danger I was in, and even with that, you came down on the side of trusting me. You really trusted me. You trusted I've got the power to make a relationship work, not just ruin it. And then I knew it wasn't only you who made things work out here. I made things work too, didn't I?"

"You did indeed. It took both of us."

"I remember you said that right from the beginning. You said I had to hold up my part of the bargain, and you would hold up yours."

"Yes, we both had to do our part."

"I know every day I have to do my part. I ask myself, do I really want the high that comes from biting people? From yelling and screaming like my family? Or do I want to know what it means to live with love, with another person? You let me go all the way to the bottom of myself to find out."

"It's so important to find that out, isn't it?"

"It is." Michelle paused and was quiet for a few moments. "I got exhausted a lot of times," she continued, "but I'm so glad I didn't give up. I had my head into all of this, I wasn't looking up, I was totally at work on all of this, and finally I saw where all the pride comes from."

"You did?"

"Yeah, I finally got it. Pride is the way my family protects themselves from the pain of not being loved. It's the only way they know how to deal with the pain, but then they just create more pain. And I was just the same, but in my own way."

"What a powerful realization."

"It was. And just when I started to deal with the pain for real, with you, who comes along in my life and waltzes in with this thing about how he's been working on pride in his family, with his Dad who's not even alive? Who else but my guy? At Ronnie's graduation, when I heard Jeff talk to me about pride, it was like I recognized him. I almost said it to him right there and then. 'I recognize you Jeff, you're my man.' It would have been too soon, but who knows, maybe not. I think we were both ready for it."

"When you saw him, you knew you were ready?"

"I did. When I saw him, I had this really strange feeling come over me, like something important was about to happen. It was really eerie. It was like time stopped. Do you know that feeling?"

"Oh yes, I do."

"When I looked at him, I just knew, oh, there's going to be a real person on the other end of the love, not the Prince of my dreams. No man is going to love you in the most ideal way. He's going to love in his way, the way that comes out of who he is. My Jeff? He's the one for me, but I have to learn to live with him as he is. He's a guy who can be dreamy some of the time, like when he gets lost in his memories. It can be annoying. I'm more down to earth. Sometimes I have to bring him back, tell him to get real. When he's off in his own little world, you just have to wait. Then he comes back. That's just the way it is. We do have little fights but not very often. And every time we do, I learn something more about myself."

"That's so important."

"It is. So I'm grateful to you, Grace. You were the one who knew I could get ready to handle a real guy and everything that comes with it. It's like you carried that for me until I could carry it for myself. Once I could carry my own load, I was ready to dial up love."

"How wonderful, Michelle."

She smiled and then her face turned serious. "It all came because I kind of borrowed a mother. That was you. That's what I needed."

I nodded.

Michelle brushed the hair out of her face and said, "It was hard. Nobody can tell you if you're ready to pay the price for looking at yourself. You let me decide if I could do it. I was the only one who could decide that." As Michelle finished talking, she folded up her collar again and looked at her pin. "Maybe I can wear it now without being too scared," she said.

We had reached the end of the session. As she left, she looked at me with that smile that stays so much in my mind. "It was ok that I borrowed you," she said. "I figured out a while ago that I could take you with me when I leave. That's ok too. You'll be with me wherever I go."

That was not the last time I saw Michelle and our work continued fruitfully for some time after that, but at the moment she said those words to me I was certain the hard part of our work together was finally behind us. The rest did prove much easier. In moments of reflection, I've thought of her often. I recall her struggles, and with a feeling of satisfaction, I recall her victories. And I often smile, as we often did together.

Chapter Nineteen—Jeff

The Office of Dr. Yoav Zein. Psychotherapy.

Hours By Appointment.

Friday, May 17, 2013.

"You remember last session I was in the middle of telling you about how Mike and I were talking about women and sex and stuff?"

"Yes, I remember."

As he settled on the sofa, Jeff said he was eager to finish telling me about his conversation with Mike at the bar, but first, he wanted me to know that the feeling of "walking in an enchanted city" had come over him again today. It was the same feeling, he reminded me, that came over him as he was strolling along with Michelle just before his surprise meeting with Mike on the street. There certainly was something about today that did seem enchanted. It was another beautiful if rather breezy day with the late-blooming tulips waving in the wind along the edge of Central Park. Once again, the city seemed to be alive in a mood of springtime elation.

"So we were sitting there at our table at the bar," he said, "and Mike was doing something I'd seen him do a hundred times before. He was playing with an empty glass with both of his hands, sliding it back and forth. It's a nervous habit of his. You remember he said he needed to reinvent himself, and he was all ears about what I might have to say? I didn't trust he really meant it. He was drinking too much like he always did and he was making those lame jokes that come with too much Scotch. There was a moment when we just seemed to run out of steam, and we weren't talking and it was awkward as hell. Then he stopped playing with his glass and he asked me a question that really zinged me."

"What did he say?"

Jeff resumed his account of what happened at the bar.

"You look down on me, don't you?" Mike asked suddenly.

"Oh God, what a question," Jeff said. "No, Mike, not now, no, I don't. If I did before, I'm sorry. Mike, I'm in no position to look down on you. You were my best friend. We shared everything. It's me who'll always be grateful for that."

"Ok, ok, you have something to say to me? I'll show you I'm really interested." Mike got up and motioned to get the attention of the barmaid and said in a loud voice, "Young lady! Cancel that next Scotch. Bring me a ginger ale, please. And one for my good buddy here." He sat back down and said, "If you've ever seen me cancel a drink, say so."

"No, I never have."

"You want proof I'm serious and I'm listening? There's your proof." They were silent until the new drinks arrived. Mike put both hands around his glass but didn't drink. "All right, you were talking about this discovery of yours, about 'raising the bar.' What's that all about?"

"It's about that I discovered that there's something behind sex and love."

"You mean that men are dogs, right?"

"It's funny that you say that. Did you ever stop to think about what was driving you to have sex?"

"No, I just went for it. The whole thing drives me crazy."

"Well, did you ever wonder what it was that was driving you crazy? I mean, was that always a good feeling?"

"No, of course not." Mike took a sip of his ginger ale and said, "Go on."

"Well, for me, I felt there was something driving me, driving me going after sex, going after women, and I had to know what that was, I reached the point where I just couldn't keep going without knowing."

"And what is it?"

"I'll tell you, but I have to put it my way."

"By all means."

"Ok, when you point to something, a dog will follow where you're pointing. I think they're the only animal that will do that. So something in me was pointing me toward just the wrong women, and toward sex in a really random way, and I just followed where I was pointed. I didn't know I was being directed. And it could direct me to things that weren't good for me. I needed to get to the point where I could say, I agree with where I'm being pointed, or I don't."

"Wait a minute, so you're agreeing men are dogs?"

"Only if we don't realize something else is in charge, and we just follow where we're pointed. But if we can say yes or no, then we take charge and we're not dogs anymore. Then we're men."

"Whew, this is what you've been doing since…" Mike didn't say it, but it was clear he meant since the friendship ended.

"Yeah. I got a hold of some things like that, things that were happening in me."

"And it makes you happy?"

"Oh definitely. It's like a huge weight's been lifted off my shoulders. I can't say I'm even close to learning all about what drives me, but I didn't want to be Mr. Compulsion. Before I started raising the bar, I wasn't making things happen in my life, and there was no way I could have made it with Michelle either. I wasn't ready."

"How did you get ready?"

"I looked at my history with women, and I saw something that shocked me."

Mike laughed and said, "I know all about that one. Ok, what shocked you, my friend?"

"I had my wires crossed. I wanted sex and love and the right woman to do something for me that I needed to do for myself first. What I really needed was to feel better about myself, but how was I going about it? I was waiting to feel better about myself, like waiting for a fish to jump out of the water right into my bucket. That was the beginning of seeing myself as I really was, facing the facts."

"Like what facts?"

"When I looked at myself, I was really shocked that if an unhappy person like me has sex, it's going to be unhappy sex."

"Isn't that kind of obvious?"

"It wasn't to me. That got me started on the path of getting ready."

"Okay, I think I get what you're saying, but that's you Jeff, that's you taking control, but do you really think everybody can do it?"

"I don't know. I'm just a beginner at it. What do you think?"

"It sounds very nice. I mean it, I'm not being cynical. But I doubt it would work for me."

"Why?"

"Because I'm not you."

"You wouldn't need to be."

"I'm not so sure."

"Well, since you asked, and you did ask, there must be some part of you that wonders like I did, right? There must be some part of you that wants to know what's going on with you and women."

"Ah, that's the old Jeff I know. Mr. Detective. Not missing a clue."

"It's true, I did look for a clue, that's how I got to why I was so frustrated, not getting what I wanted with women."

"Wait, you didn't say what the clue was."

"It's that every time I had sex, there was something driving me into it and that something wanted something, something it wasn't getting."

"What did it want?"

"It wanted me to connect to the other person. Be enough of a person to get all I could from it. I found out connecting is where the magic happens in life. We need that more than anything. But if we're not enough of a person, and the woman we're with isn't enough of a person, then the thing that gave us all that energy to hook up, that thing isn't satisfied. It didn't get what it wanted and needed. No connection, no satisfaction. I could keep looking for a lifetime, and another lifetime, and it wouldn't be there. That's why I was so frustrated."

"I always thought frustration and sex go together."

"That's what I thought too. But with Michelle, with what I have now, connecting takes me beyond myself, it's the greatest thing in the world when it goes well. I need that and I'm going for that, and when it happens I'm on top of the world. I really like myself when I make the connection happen, I like being alive, but at the same time I've finally got my feet on the ground. I see what's going on most of the time. That's where my life wanted to take me all along. Connected to myself. It's how I was meant to live."

With that, Jeff stopped his account of the conversation, stretched, rearranged himself on the sofa, and said, "You know I wasn't about to tell Mike that being on top of the world isn't the whole story."

"What do you mean?" I asked.

"We were just sort of getting to know each other again so I didn't want to tell him about how I had to raise my bar to deal with the other side of Michelle, the challenges. That was more private."

"Not something you wanted to share?"

"Right. Later maybe, but not yet. Anyway, he knows too much already about the difficult side of dealing with women. I didn't need to tell him about Michelle's rough side, the one where's she's like a wounded animal when her sore spots are touched. I know I'll probably always have to deal with that side of her, but it really helped that I caught on that I can stand firm and not lose it even when she does things I don't like. Overcoming obstacles is part of the whole picture."

"That's true, isn't it?"

"It is," Jeff said. "So I didn't tell him about the private stuff, but I did say a lot of what I've been through."

Jeff returned to his account of the conversation at the bar. After Jeff's comment about where his life had led him, Mike was again pushing his glass back and forth on the table. "Are you saying that's why I chase women?" he asked. "I'm looking for a connection and I'm not finding it?"

"I think so," Jeff said.

Mike was silent for a very long time. He started to speak and then stopped. He looked around the bar and seemed about to call for the barmaid again but then turned back. He rocked back and forth in his seat, thinking to himself. Then he said, "What about friendship? Is that about connecting too?"

"Oh yeah, it's gotta be true there too," Jeff said.

"So have you learned anything about that?"

"Whoa, that's the old Mike I know, not afraid to go for the jugular."

"I'm serious, I want to know. Did you learn anything about friendship?"

Jeff took his time answering. "Look," he said, "I have this problem. Everything I might say sounds corny when I say it, but not when I think it."

"So say it," Mike said. "I don't mind corny."

"Wasn't there always something bigger than both of us in our friendship? Doesn't that stay on, even if we lost track of it?"

"We both lost track of a lot of things," Mike said. He pushed his drink away and put his hands on the table. "Don't stop me now, just listen. Back then, I said a lot of things to you that I should've never said. I did it a lot of times too. You were damn right to stop talking to me, I'm amazed you're even talking to me now. I did screw up my marriage and I screwed up my friendship with you. I really missed the boat and there's no excuse. I have to live with it."

There was a long silence.

"I almost called you a lot of times," Mike said, his head down and his hands still on the table.

"I almost called you a lot of times, too," Jeff said. "I don't know why I never did it. I did think a lot about what you would say if we talked."

Mike looked up. "You did? Like talking to me in your head?" he said. "What did I say?"

"You said hang in there, buddy, don't get discouraged, don't let your frustration get the better of you. Be determined."

"Hey, I make a lot of sense when I'm talking in your head, don't I?"

"You do."

"Man, how did we ever…"

As before, the unspoken meaning of Mike's sentence was clear.

"What you said about water under the bridge? I'm up for that," Jeff said. "It's best to let go of the past, but if there's anything I've learned in the last few years, it's that you can repair more about past relationships than I thought."

Once again, Jeff stopped his account of the conversation and said to me, "You've probably guessed what I was thinking right then?"

"I'm not sure," I said, "What were you thinking?"

"I was thinking about how I repaired my relationship with my Dad even after he was gone. If I made that happen, I was wondering how far I could go with something just like that, but with Mike."

"What did you come up with?"

"From what I did with my Dad, I feel like I found something reliable in myself. It was like I brought my Dad here so he could get some therapy too, something he couldn't have gotten by himself. I brought us closer. It's an accomplishment and I'm kind of proud I made that happen."

"With good reason."

"Yeah, so while I was talking with Mike, I was thinking, hey if that could happen with my Dad, why couldn't things get better with Mike too? How far could I push it? I was wondering, is there any way to know beforehand or do you just have to try?"

"I see."

"I thought, be realistic, you can't repair everything in life. Mike is alive, my Dad is not. I was really on the fence about Mike, like who was he now, was he different? Was there room for something new in the friendship, or maybe not?"

"What did you decide?"

"These days when I need to feel sure about something I come back to me, myself. Ok, forget about Mike for a minute, what about me? What do I know about that question he asked me? Have I learned anything about friendship?"

"What was your answer?"

"I do know something about how to repair things in myself, and that does change everything about how I feel about my life, but it's also so strange that people aren't the same when you change inside. You have to leave room for that too. There can be more to them than what you saw before. That's what I learned."

With that statement of Jeff's, a wave of contentment came over me. Our work together had played an indispensable role in bringing him many good things in life, things that were just what was wanted and needed. A good job, a good wife, and perhaps now a restored friendship. My contentment stemmed from the way he was on his own two feet, living "right side up" with himself, as he put it. The ups and downs of life would continue, of course, but so would his creative way of dealing with them. He spoke, and I was brought back from those thoughts.

"With Mike, I found out right away I could push things a lot more than I thought."

"How so?"

"After I said I've learned about repairing relationships, Mike seemed really happy. He was smiling like the old Mike. It felt great."

"What did he say?"

Jeff resumed telling me of the conversation at the bar.

"So I take it you're one of those 'love yourself' people?" Mike asked.

"Yes, in my own way. You've got to have that before you can get to love with another person. Mike, if you don't like yourself, how can you expect things to go well with somebody else?"

"Another great truth from my old friend." Mike was playing with a half-empty glass again. "I remember I didn't like wondering if you liked me."

Jeff took a deep breath. "Wow Mike, that's really brave of you to say."

There was silence and Mike started pushing the glass around again. Jeff said, "The most honest thing I can say is that I like you now."

"You didn't before?"

"I don't think I really saw you before." Jeff paused and said, "In fact, I know I didn't."

"Well, like I said, we both got off track, didn't we?"

"Yeah, I know for sure I did," Jeff said.

Once again, Mike pushed his glass back and forth. "So maybe it was the right time for both of us to run into each other," he said. As before, he rocked back and forth to his own thoughts. "And your wife?" he said. "Did she have to make herself ready to be with you?"

"That was true for Michelle too." There was a long silence. "Listen, Mike," Jeff said, "I know you can't just take my word for it, you always say you're into proof. So am I."

"What kind of proof are you talking about?"

"The kind where the proof is in yourself."

"What on earth does that mean?"

"Ok, so I already told you how we had to get to the right place in ourselves before we could get together, right?"

"Yeah."

"And I told you how there wasn't much going on about our love life for each of us, and what we had to do to make things change?"

"Yeah, yeah."

"But I know the story of how it happened isn't the proof for anybody else. It never can be."

"Why not?"

"Because the only kind of proof that counts is what's alive in a person. It's what you've actually lived that proves it to you. Michelle and I, we're the living proof."

"Proof of what?"

"Proof that if you're messed up when your life starts, love might be out of reach, but that doesn't have to be the end of the story."

ABOUT THE AUTHOR

David Rottman (**david@davidrottman.com**) is Past President and Chairman of the Board of the C.G. Jung Foundation of New York.

He is a Faculty Member of the Jung Foundation's Continuing Education Program and has taught courses on Jungian Psychology for more than 25 years. He has a private practice in New York City

Made in the USA
Middletown, DE
17 February 2020

84913504R00128